7F LD

His body was the beautiful, smoothly sculpted work of a driven man

A grin pulled at Cash's mouth, but didn't reach his eyes. He tugged at the towel around his waist and freed it, first rubbing at his stomach and then at his chest.

Reine was speechless. Was that his aim? To silence her? To drive her away?

"What is it you expect me to do, Reine?" Cash finally asked, casually holding the towel between them. "Rant and rail at the gods?" His brow furrowed. "Or pay the ransom?"

She shook her head. "I don't know what I expected from you—"

"Then why did you come?"

"Because I figured, despite everything you might still care, just a little."

"About Gray?" he asked. "Or you?"

He dropped the towel....

Dear Reader,

A hero or heroine without any faults would make pretty dull reading since the most gripping conflicts come, not from outside forces, but from within.

The Seven Deadly Sins—Pride, Sloth, Lust, Greed, Anger, Envy and Gluttony—exemplify the most hurtful behavior, human failings that can keep us locked in self-absorption and self-doubt. They can keep us from finding real happiness within ourselves...or with that one special person whom we all deserve....

As a writer, I love nothing more than throwing my heroes and heroines to the precipice of danger, to make ordinary people fight the worst villains and win. For me, it's a celebration of the human spirit, the discovery of untapped strengths that I am certain we all possess if only we can find the courage to reach deep inside ourselves.

For SEVEN SINS, I've chosen to raise the stakes, to push my heroes and heroines to the emotional edge at the same time they are fighting for their very existence. In the midst of mortal danger, they must wrestle with equally destructive inner demons and take back their lives...and in doing so, be rewarded with a love for all time.

Let me know how you enjoy their stories at P.O. Box 578279, Chicago, IL 60657-8297.

Patricia Rosemoor

Cowboy Justice
Patricia Rosemoor

HARLEQUIN®

TORONTO • NEW YORK • LONDON
AMSTERDAM • PARIS • SYDNEY • HAMBURG
STOCKHOLM • ATHENS • TOKYO • MILAN • MADRID
PRAGUE • WARSAW • BUDAPEST • AUCKLAND

To Linda,
For the one that I missed.

ISBN 0-373-22530-X

COWBOY JUSTICE

Printed in U.S.A.

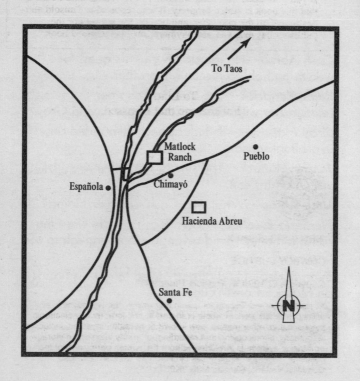

To Taos

Matlock
Ranch

Pueblo

Española

Chimayó

Hacienda Abreu

Santa Fe

N

CAST OF CHARACTERS

Cash Abreu—He reluctantly put his quest for wealth on hold to rescue his brother.

Reine Kendrick—She tried to keep her relationship with Cash strictly about saving Gray.

Gray Matlock—His kidnappers demanded an exorbitant ransom.

Jasper Matlock—The sins of the father were being visited on his son.

Luna Abreu—What was Cash's mother hiding?

Nemesio Escobar—Could Cash's uncle want the ransom money—and revenge—bad enough to see Gray die?

Evan Bixler—He'd already tried to get his hands on Matlock Construction.

Sam Valdez—He believed the Matlock's river property was stolen from his family.

Selena Cullen—Matlock had financially ruined her son, who then committed suicide.

Prologue

''So, we've arrived at the midpoint of our collaboration,'' Zoe Declue told her writing partner as he took the chair upholstered in nubby cream with ivory-satin stripes. The seating area near the windows would be more comfortable, but more than ever, she was feeling the need to keep her desk between them. ''Sin number four.''

Pride, Sloth, Lust, Avarice, Envy, Wrath, Gluttony—the humanistic ramifications of the Seven Deadly Sins in individual lives had absorbed her since she'd taken her first psych course. As a research psychologist, she'd spent years gathering as much information on the subject as she could.

And her position here at Haven, a privately funded mental-health foundation, gave her the opportunity to turn that knowledge into a useful tool for the lay person—with help from one very talented writer.

From his charcoal slacks and buttoned-up-to-the-throat silk shirt to his glowering visage, Alex Gotham presented the only dark spot in her office, which was a study in the same pale neutral colors that she preferred for herself.

Shifting under his stare, she asked, "Is something wrong?"

"'Midpoint'..." he echoed. "You're keeping score."

"I'm tracking our progress."

Zoe eyed the growing manuscript on her desk—the first three chapters of their proposed self-help book that would deal with the Seven Deadly Sins. Now that they were starting work on number four, they were approaching the halfway mark—quite a thrilling accomplishment, as far as she was concerned.

Alex didn't look equally thrilled when he said, "You're anxious for it to be over."

She met his dark gaze. "Aren't you?"

"I wouldn't put it *that* way. Sounds like you'll be glad to be rid of me."

"Oh...I didn't mean to be insensitive...."

Zoe let her words trail off as she noted a twitch around his lips and realized that Alex was baiting her again, an increasingly frequent occurrence. Warmth crept through her and she tried covering it by hooking her blunt chin-length hair behind an ear and sorting through a pile of folders, although "Avarice" was already on top.

It had taken her some time to realize that Alex often said things merely to get a reaction out of her. She wasn't used to working with someone she had such difficulty reading. In the beginning, she'd assessed Alex as uptight, and seeming to need to prove something—to himself, or to the world.

Sometimes she still got glimpses of that man below the more easygoing surface that had emerged. Certain that this was the real Alex, she had to wonder what, exactly, had happened to make him go underground for nearly two years.

Knowing that her own writing was too erudite for a broad audience, Zoe had sought him out after reading *Lost Youth,* his critically acclaimed glimpse into the world of runaway teens. For a while, his book had given him celebrity...and then he'd disappeared from the public eye. Literally. Still, she'd wanted to enlist his talent and so had made it her business to find him. It had never occurred to her that they would become more than collaborators. But lately, she'd recognized a stronger bond being formed between them.

Friendship? she wondered, a bit uneasily.

And what would be wrong with that? Her entire humanistic theory of the seven sins had to do with isolation—that of an individual being guilty of a crime against his- or herself, and therefore preventing himself or herself from forming a true bond with society, not to mention from establishing personal relationships.

Not having such a relationship of her own—currently, she was too busy to see anyone socially—Zoe quickly turned away from that last thought.

"Avarice," she began, opening the folder she'd separated from the pile. "The willingness to climb over others to get to the top... Loving the idea of possessing more than the possessions themselves... Making possessions of people."

Like the other chapters, this one would focus on an individual who'd found a second chance at life after having conquered one of the emotion-based sins. Thank heaven for her cooperative colleagues across the country and their generous patients who had given written permission for their stories to be used. These individuals would remain anonymous as agreed upon, but they, too, could take reward in knowing that they would help so many other people with similar problems.

"Greed. A tough one," Alex said. "Hard to forgive, especially the 'treating people like possessions' part. You actually found a story you think readers can identify with?"

"I hope so. Given his circumstances, Cash Abreu's affinity for greed was understandable if not justifiable."

"How so?"

"He was the son of the laundress and foreman on the Matlock spread in New Mexico. Jasper Matlock treated him abusively—"

"He beat the kid?"

"No. At least, not until the day Matlock drove him from the ranch and told him never to return."

"And did he?"

Zoe nodded. "Cash came back for his father's funeral. That's how the whole thing started. And this is how it almost ended."

She handed Alex a newspaper clipping with the headline: Land Magnate's Only Son Disappears....

Chapter One

Wednesday

The soft glow of sunset hovered over the Chimayo Valley as Grayson Matlock loped his mustang along the eroded barranca in search of a stray calf. A hawk wheeled along the spinelike ridge that seemed incandescent, reminding him of adobe when lit by the burning coals of a kiva fireplace.

He brought his mount to a stop, stood in his stirrups and checked the badlands that bordered the verdant valley like long, rugged arms.

Where was that little bugger?

The calf was a naughty one, always wandering away from his mama's side to explore. Gray had nicknamed him Wanderlust, a capricious holdover from the days of his childhood when he'd refused to think about what would happen to the cattle raised on the Matlock Ranch.

His daddy had always reminded him, though, had always told him he was too soft—if not in body, then in heart. Jasper Matlock had maintained that a man shouldn't get involved with an animal who might someday be staring up at him from his dinner plate.

But Gray had anyway, and he'd tried not to think of the fate of the creatures he'd befriended.

He urged his mount on, toward a nearby box canyon, the site of an old, abandoned chile mill.

The years hadn't changed him. Nor had his taking over the running of the ranch. Hired hands and neighbors alike might chuckle over what they considered his soft attitude—a man could have a worse reputation, Gray knew—but while the herd was in his care, he considered its hooved members more than commodities. And while he couldn't know each and every one of them, a few cows or calves with personality always caught his attention.

Like Wanderlust.

Entering the canyon along a barely wet streambed, Gray frowned. Considering the calf had been out of sight of the rest of the herd for a while now, this was far, even for the most curious of creatures.

And Wanderlust was such a little guy....

Instincts kicking in, Gray felt his suspicions rise along with the walls around him. Maybe the calf hadn't wandered off at all...or at least, not this far on his own.

Gray's sudden shock of uncertainty transmitted to his mount, for the mustang started dancing.

Gray ran a hand along the ragged mane. "It's all right, son," he murmured.

But Gray couldn't settle down inside. Nor could he turn back before he'd finished checking out the canyon.

They came out of nowhere. Two of them. Armed. Rifles aimed straight at him.

They were wearing hoods beneath their hats, as if covering their faces would hide their identities when one of them hadn't even bothered to switch from his usual mount. Gray might not be able to identify every head of cattle in the area, but he was familiar with most of the horses.

When had they taken to rustling? he wondered. "You boys on your way to a masquerade party?" he asked in as conversational a tone as he could manage.

"Yep," one of them drawled, raising his rifle to his shoulder. "And you're the damned guest of honor."

Thursday

"I WANT THAT LAND," Cash Abreu growled into the receiver, aggravated by another failed attempt. He leaned back in his chair, put his feet up on the mesquite desk and noted the scrape across the toe of one of his handmade boots. His temper rising, he snarled, "I thought we had a deal."

"I'm holding up my end of the bargain. But for now, it's a no go."

"You can be a no go, as well."

"That'd be your decision, Abreu. Hey, as long as I get my money...one way or the other...."

Cash heard the threat in the other man's tone, but managed to hold his anger in check. He needed allies if he was going to succeed in his promise to Jasper Matlock—even allies he had to pay.

Finally too close to his goal to take a stumble, he said, "The deal stands as made."

"I figured it might."

"We'll get another chance at him," Cash promised, already figuring out how best to proceed. "And soon."

He hung up and set his feet on the floor. The scraped boot glared up at him. Now he'd have to get a duplicate pair made. Not that he didn't have a couple of dozen others to choose from, and not that he'd give a second thought to the cost. But these were his favorites and they were broken in exactly the way he liked them.

"Are you busy?" came a soft voice from behind.

"Never too busy for you, Mom," Cash said as he swiveled toward her.

Luna Abreu stood in the doorway of his home office. While small in stature and compact, as were most women of Pueblo-Hispanic descent, she filled the room with her presence and her exotic beauty. He knew she still had the power to draw a man to her with a glance of her sparkling dark eyes, because he'd seen it happen more than once. Her face was unlined, ageless, the silver wings threading through her coiled black hair the only suggestion that she'd left her fiftieth birthday behind.

Cash rose, stooping to envelop her in a big hug. "I thought you were taking the day off."

His mother never had to lift a finger again as far as he was concerned. He'd had enough money to support her in style for nearly a decade now, but she refused to be useless. She ran his home for him with the help of Gloria—a young "maid-in-training"— and an elderly groundsman who moved so slowly that no one else would employ him. But Ignacio was a case in point, his mother had insisted when she'd hired the man, saying he would go off somewhere and die if he didn't feel useful.

Thank God Cash hadn't inherited her sentimentality.

"I planned on doing some shopping in Chimayo," she said. "Some new weavings…" Her fingers grasped at his sleeves so he couldn't move away from her. "But in town, I heard— Well, i-it's just a rumor—still, I wanted to tell you myself.…"

His mother's sudden case of nerves unsettled Cash. He stiffened.

"Tell me what?"

"Something terrible may have happened." She looked up at him, her gaze sober. "It's Gray. Word is…he's disappeared."

"MY GOD, WHY DOESN'T IT ring?"

"Get a hold of yourself, woman!" Jasper Matlock snapped, even as he paced the length of the huge living room too fancy for his taste. He'd be damned if he'd take his boots off in his own home, no matter the color or cost of the carpet. "Stop imagining the worst!"

Swollen-eyed and red-nosed, Marlene sat on the shadowy side of the room, staring at the telephone. She'd spent half the night and the whole morning weeping and they didn't even know a thing yet.

He himself had been alarmed, of course, when his son's horse had come back riderless the night before. The men he'd sent to scout the area hadn't seen anything in the dark. More had ridden out at dawn, had even picked up and followed the mustang's tracks to the riverbed where they'd lost them. They'd kept looking anyhow.

Had found nothing.

A fresh search party with an experienced tracker had been out there since noon, but in his gut, Jasper feared they'd find more of the same—who knew how far they'd followed the river?

Better that than a body, an evil voice inside his head whispered.

Gray, dead... His worst fear.

What could have happened? How could he have up and disappeared without a trace?

A thought struck him....

Cash!

But the seething flow of his mind was interrupted by a tense, "I think we should call the sheriff."

He jerked to a stop and glared at his wife's niece, as usual all prim and proper, heavy blond hair coiled at the base of her neck, lace-edged blouse buttoned up to her chin. At the first sniff of trouble, Reine Kendrick had come running to stick her nose where it didn't belong. Also as usual.

"Mind your own business, girl. I don't know what you're doing here anyhow. Don't you have some troubled teenagers to ride herd on?"

"Not today. Gray *is* my business," Reine said firmly. "And Aunt Marlene needs me."

She placed a hand on his wife's shoulder and gave him one of those defiant looks that had always irritated the hell out of him from the day they'd taken her in.

"If I'd known how much trouble you were gonna be—"

"You would have left me to the nuns. Yes, I know," Reine said quietly, though she was unable to cover a bitterness that hadn't always been there. "You've reminded me often enough."

And well he should have.

Jasper's troubles had all started with his wife's

niece, he reminded himself. Not that he hated the girl. In the best of times, he'd almost thought of Reine as the daughter Marlene couldn't give him. But this wasn't anywhere close to a good day. And his memory was long, his nature unforgiving. If not for his trying to protect her...

The telephone rang.

Marlene reached for it, but Jasper snatched it right out from under his wife's hand. "Who is this?" he demanded, praying one of his men had had a reason to use the cell phone he'd thrust at them.

"Jasper Matlock, land magnate?" said the sexless, altered voice from the receiver.

His heart thundered. "Speaking." Though "magnate" had become an exaggeration of his current financial state.

"Jasper," Marlene hissed at him.

Fingers gripping the receiver, he ignored her and concentrated on the voice.

"Your son is safe...*for now*...so keep it to yourself, if you get my drift."

No sheriff, then.

"What is it you want?" Jasper demanded, now shrugging off the hand that clawed at his arm.

"You'll be hearing from me," the disembodied voice promised.

"When?"

But the caller had already hung up.

He threw the receiver into its cradle.

"Was that about Gray or not?" Marlene demanded, her voice anguished.

Nodding absently, he pulled a hand through silver hair.

"Shoulda known," he muttered. "Gray's been snatched for ransom. Someone's out to ruin me!"

"Is that all you care about?" Marlene's still-beautiful features twisted as she shoved him in the chest with both hands. "Your precious money?"

Doubly shocked, Jasper stared at his distraught wife. "Sometimes I wonder if you know me at all, woman!"

Still, considering his current circumstances, Jasper couldn't help but worry about *how much* ransom would be required for the safe return of what had always been his most precious possession.

AT SUNSET, REINE STOPPED her car practically within spitting distance of Hacienda Abreu—well, within shouting distance, anyway—and waited for her stomach to settle. The last thing in the world she'd ever thought she would do was to approach Cash for a favor after all these years.

Not that she was afraid of facing him; those old feelings were long gone. He'd driven them from her heart as he himself had been driven from Matlock Ranch.

It was just that he'd become a man she couldn't respect. Hard. Ruthless. Greedy.

Another Jasper Matlock.

The setting sun fired the pinnacles and spires of the barrancas jutting out from the valley beyond the house, making her realize that a full twenty-four hours had passed since Gray had gone after the stray.

Reminding herself of the boy Cash had once been—of the feelings he'd once had for Gray—Reine took heart, and started her car.

She worked on positive thoughts as she wended

her way along a gravel road through the chamiso and golden aspens toward the real adobe home that Cash had built years after buying the land neighboring Matlock Ranch. Reine suspected he'd wanted to be right under Jasper's nose, to throw his success in the old man's face.

He'd done a damn fine job of it, too.

She pulled up opposite the front entrance and slid out of the car.

Hacienda Abreu's exterior was fortresslike but for the shaded, Saltillo-tiled front porch with wide ponderosa-pine beams. She'd barely stepped a booted toe onto it when she came face-to-face with a suspended swing of weathered wood that could have come straight out of her adolescence. Her breath caught in her throat. There'd been one just like it on the Matlock Ranch. She and Cash had spent hours swinging together, playing guessing games about what the future might hold for them....

She couldn't help herself. Grasping the seat, she gave it a small push to see if it would creak.

The familiar sound sent a shiver up her spine and her racing for the front door.

There was no bell or buzzer. With a hand that trembled slightly, she clanked the gecko-shaped knocker, then stepped back and crossed her arms over her chest.

A moment later, the door opened to reveal a young Hispanic woman in jeans and a T-shirt, hands held up around her face like a surgeon, elbow-length rubber gloves dripping soapy water.

"I'm here to see Cash," Reine said. "Mr. Abreu."

"He's probably holed up in his office. Um…" The girl's long black ponytail swung over her shoulder as she glanced down at the suds on the tile floor. She tried blotting the wet spots with her bare feet. "Give me a sec and I'll get him."

Thinking the advantage of surprise wouldn't hurt her case, Reine said, "No, wait, I didn't mean to interrupt you at your work. Just point the way and I'll find him myself."

The girl gave her an intent look, then said, "Yeah, sure. You look safe enough. That way." Her indicating the direction with a gloved hand dripped more suds in another area. She muttered something to herself in Spanish, then to Reine said, "Around the corner and through the living area. The office is the only room on the left near the hall. Can't miss it."

"Thanks."

Equilibrium restored, Reine swept through an arched doorway into the two-story living area that had been decorated with some of the finest-crafted Southwestern furniture she'd ever seen. She especially appreciated the *trastero,* a tall wooden cupboard, with a raised Native American pattern on its doors. At the far end of the room was a hallway.

And just before it, the office was, indeed, impossible to miss.

It was also empty.

Reine glanced back, but the young woman had disappeared. Hesitating for only a second, she stepped inside. Niches carved into plaster walls on either side of a corner beehive fireplace provided shelving for books. A hand-carved desk sat before windows facing the inner courtyard, the center of which she could see was graced by a tiered fountain.

"My heart flows over…my spirit flies…."

Snatches of soft country music beckoned from another part of the house and drifted through an open doorway to her right. Figuring if she followed the sound, she would find Cash, Reine decided to investigate further. Entering a wide hallway that was being used as a gallery, she slowed and turned in a circle, eyes opening in amazement at the collection of Southwestern artists on the walls, including Gorman and Peña and a small O'Keeffe—all originals.

"Long, lonesome road…called love…"

A little awed by the museum-quality gallery that was part of Cash's home, Reine felt another surge of nerves as she kept going through the only other open door. After taking several steps into the room, she froze. Cash's bedroom. His king-size, raw-pine four-poster bed was unmade. The turquoise-and-clay-colored sheets and matching quilt were rumpled as if he'd been napping. And from an inner room, the rush of running water competed with the sounds coming from his CD player.

"…never thought I'd see you…again.…"

Both the music and the sound of the water died at the same time, startling Reine. Her pulse fluttering strangely, she wondered what the heck she was doing stalking Cash in the privacy of his own bedroom. She should have let the girl find him—or at the very least have waited in his office.

His office…

She should go there now.

But she'd scarcely backed up a step before a door opened and Cash stepped out.

Reine started at the sight before her—a long expanse of damp skin covering a powerfully-built body—and a rush of something familiar and forbidden enveloped her. Even realizing he'd wrapped a turquoise towel around his trim waist didn't dissipate the primitive response that set her pulse racing and stole her breath. His bronzed skin mesmerized her as did the wet tendrils of dark hair brushing his forehead.

When Cash finally spotted her, a flicker of surprise crossed his features, but he kept coming past the bed, stopping with barely a yard between them. His dark eyes seemed to devour her, touching the lace at her throat, the silver-and-turquoise button covers on the front of her blouse, the Concho belt wrapped around her waist, the folds of deep blue velvet skirt flowing down over her thighs to the tops of her boots.

"Didn't know I had company."

"I didn't know you were otherwise occupied." She hated the catch in her voice. "Your cleaning girl said you'd be in your office."

"She was obviously mistaken since this *obviously* isn't my office."

"I just followed the music...."

Feeling awkward and foolish and not knowing where to look, Reine let her words trail off and locked onto his gaze for safety—such as it was. His suddenly intense expression made her doubly uncomfortable.

Why was he looking at her like that?

Why now?

They'd seen each other over the years more than a dozen times, usually at some public or charitable function. He'd always had a woman on his arm, always blond, each one more beautiful than the last.

But they'd never spoken then.

She started to back away. "I—I can wait for you in your office."

''You're here now. Have your say.''

But with him so close she could almost feel the heat of his skin, she was having trouble thinking, let alone talking. Still, her mission was important, so she doubled her effort.

''It's about Gray,'' she managed.

''He hasn't shown up yet?''

''You already know?''

''Only that he disappeared last night,'' he said in a purely conversational tone.

Cash was acting so casually—as if it didn't mean anything to him, as if Gray didn't... It threw her off anew.

When she said, ''He's been kidnapped,'' Reine noted barely a flicker in Cash's gaze. She kept silent for a moment, waiting for a response that didn't come. ''Aren't you going to say *anything?*''

''What would you like me to say?''

''Something. That you're sorry. That you can't believe this is happening. That you want to help. For heaven's sake, Gray is your brother!''

Another flicker. ''We were never brothers.''

''You can't deny your own blood.''

''No?'' Cash arched his dark eyebrows. ''That's not *my* experience.''

Damn Uncle Jasper, anyway! Reine thought furiously.

''You know that wasn't Gray's doing,'' Reine reminded him. ''And if nothing else, you were best friends!''

''A lifetime ago.''

''I don't care how long ago. You have a memory.''

But whether or not he still had a heart was another question.

His lids drooped, hooding his eyes. "I remember everything, Reine."

She hated the way he said her name—so possessively—when he didn't have the right.

"So do I, Cash, but this isn't about us."

"You could make it about us."

"Excuse me?"

A grin pulled at his mouth but didn't reach his eyes. He tugged at the towel and freed it, first rubbing at his stomach and then at his chest, where the dry air had already finished the job.

Reine was so appalled she was speechless.

Was that his aim?

To silence her? To drive her away?

Certainly not to seduce her. If Cash had wanted her, he would have made the opportunity happen. Or tried. Only he never had.

She was equally appalled by her own reaction. Having no say over her own body, her own psyche, both of which were responding to his blatant actions, she only hoped he couldn't tell.

"What is it you expect me to do, Reine?" Cash finally asked, casually holding the towel between them. "Rant and rail at the gods?" His brow furrowed. "Or pay the ransom?"

"We don't even know how much they want yet." Realizing she'd made a big mistake in coming to him, she shook her head. "And I don't even know what I expected from you—"

"Then why *did* you come?"

Reine's laugh was brittle. "Because I figured, despite everything, you might still care, just a little."

"About Gray?" he asked, pausing for only a second before adding, "Or you?"

He dropped the towel.

First, she gasped. And then she got angry.

With as much contempt as she could muster, Reine glared at Cash and gave him a thorough once-over as he so obviously was daring her to do.

His body was the beautiful, smoothly sculpted work of a driven man. And it was definitely aroused. She purposely gave *that* part of his anatomy a more thorough inspection.

Steeling herself against responding in any way that would satisfy him, she spat, "Go to hell, Cash Abreu!"

"Been there, done that."

"Obviously not long enough to learn anything!"

That said, Reine spun on her boot heel, and only with utmost will, walked rather than ran out of the room, away from the selfish bastard who had once held her heart in his hands.

CASH WAITED UNTIL REINE was out of hearing range before cursing a blue streak that would have made a cowpoke's ears burn. What the hell had possessed her to make herself at home, waltzing into his bedroom as if she owned it? Facing him down as if she owned him? He waited for the faint sound of her car starting up before moving from the spot.

Crossing the room, he threw open the double doors of his private patio and dived into the pool where he slashed his arms through the water like a windmill. He swam without pausing until his lungs ached and he couldn't drive his muscles to carry him another yard.

Gasping, he stumbled out of the water and fell onto the sun-warmed tile, where he rolled over onto his back and tried to convince himself he wasn't the bastard of all time.

He'd accomplished what he'd been after, he reminded himself—her immediate departure.

Her arrival today had thrown him.

And her update about Gray…

Against his will, he remembered the past, the day he'd dared set foot on Matlock property only months after being booted off. Matlock had found him with Reine and had beaten him before sending on his way with a warning to never return.

But no one could have kept him from his daddy's funeral.

Zane Abreu had been the father every kid dreamed of. Loving. Supportive. A friend as well as a parent. His death had devastated Cash. And so had the letter his daddy had left behind.

Cash still remembered the words he'd read so many times:

> …you have to know the truth. I married your mother because I'd loved her for years…and despite the fact that she was carrying another man's child. Jasper Matlock is the man who sired you, Son, and Gray is your half brother. Forgive me for being selfish enough to keep this secret for so many years. I love you more than my own life…

Stunned, Cash hadn't wanted to believe it, but his mother had confirmed the awful facts. Matlock had slept with her but had married Marlene; then he'd pushed Luna and Zane together.

Because she'd become inconvenient, Cash had realized, Matlock had for all intents and purposes sold off the woman he'd used. The bastard had treated his mother as if she'd been his personal slave.

That truth had echoed through Cash's head as Zane Abreu's casket had been lowered into the ground. Even as he'd said goodbye to the man who'd raised him as his own, he had seethed with the knowledge. And then, his heart breaking, he had thrown it in Jasper Matlock's face right there at the gravesite, before God and everyone.

His stomach had twisted into a sick knot. He wanted to use his fists on the man...but more than that, he wanted to hurt him in the worst possible way he knew.

"I'll make you pay!" Cash had promised the sorry bastard. "If it's the last thing I ever do, I'll strip you of everything you care about!"

And so he had over the years, to the very best of his abilities.

Cash wiped a hand over his wet face as if he could wipe away the memories. They were always there, just below the surface, waiting. He couldn't soften, couldn't allow himself to be swayed from his purpose.

He couldn't think about the past.

Therein lay danger. A threat to his plan.

He needed to stay focused if he was to get everything he'd ever wanted.

Money was his mantra.

Money made him who he was.

As did things. And land.

Except for the Matlock Ranch.

The one thing in life that he really wanted, that really would mean something to him, continued to elude him. He didn't need the water rights since he didn't raise cattle. He wasn't planning on turning the land into yet another housing development. He merely wanted to possess the acreage to prove that he could.

It irked him that he hadn't yet been able to rip the spread from Matlock's tightfisted grasp.

Maybe now…when the old man was vulnerable…

An image of Gray as a boy—his unusually fierce expression when defending their friendship—got in the way.

Keep the goal in mind, Cash reminded himself. The land.

Not the people.

Not the bodies he'd have to climb over to get it. He couldn't think about them.

Couldn't think about Gray.

Gray would be all right, he assured himself. Jasper Matlock wouldn't let a hair on his legitimate son's head be harmed.

Another memory came—of a serious little girl with golden braids touching the bloody pad of her thumb to Gray's and his as they all swore allegiance to each other.

All for one and one for all…

He couldn't think about Reine.

Especially not about Reine.

But he couldn't stop.

He'd never forget the first time she'd looked at him with a sense of awareness, and he'd realized she was seeing him as more than a best friend.

Reine had been beautiful then, but she'd grown into an even more lovely, desirable woman, the perfume she wore conjuring images of lovemaking in an exotic garden. Even while he'd been trying to shock her into leaving, his body had betrayed him.

His body was betraying him now, just remembering.

Cursing another blue streak, Cash rolled over and dropped back into the pool.

Making the Matlock Ranch his would be his new mantra.

He swam as if his very life depended on it....

Chapter Two

"I tried my best, Aunt Marlene," Reine said that night, "but Cash did't want to get involved." She realized her uncle had walked into the room in time to hear.

Jasper Matlock froze near the settee that looked too fragile to support him. He was nearly as tall as Cash, and nearly as broad-chested. That was where the physical resemblance ended, however.

Red-faced, he was glaring at her. "You went to see that good-for-nothing—"

"Blame me!" Marlene interrupted. "I asked her to go."

That wasn't exactly accurate, though Reine wasn't about to correct her aunt. Confronting Cash had been her own idea, but Marlene hadn't tried talking her out of it. Now she was being protective when there was no need.

"What did you two expect to accomplish?" Jasper demanded. "Did you think he'd roll over and play dead, maybe offer to the pay the ransom?"

Assuming they ever found out how much it was. The kidnapper hadn't yet called back with a dollar amount—a fact that Reine didn't want to examine too closely. Meanwhile, the inability to do anything positive toward assuring Gray's safety had them all on edge.

"Jasper, is there a need to go to someone else for money?" Marlene asked, a thread of fear in her voice. "I—I know the business has been worrying you for some time now. But how b-bad is it?"

Her aunt was none too steady. Her face was pale, her trembling hands matched her voice. The strain had taken its toll on her. Reine knew people often thought they were sisters rather than aunt and niece, but no one would ever make that mistake tonight. Tonight, Marlene Matlock appeared far older than her fifty-seven years.

"There may not be a need to pay the ransom at all," Jasper stated with satisfaction.

Reine's hopes rose. "You went to the sheriff?"

"Hell, no! I told you they said not to!"

"Then what are you talking about?" Marlene demanded.

"I been thinking on it—who would have reason to snatch Gray and why." He was pacing, talking more to himself than to them. "Only one person."

Apprehensive, Reine asked, "You have a theory?"

He stopped in front of her, stared her straight in the eye. "Look to Cash Abreu. What you shoulda been doin' there, girl, was askin' him where my son is stashed."

"*Our* son," Marlene reminded him from where she huddled on the sofa.

"Uncle Jasper, why would you think Cash knows anything about it?" His implication appalled Reine.

"The land." Jasper socked a fist into his open

hand. "He's been after my spread for years. Maybe he got tired of waitin' and figured himself out a plan."

"You can't possibly believe he would use Gray!"

"Why not? He's capable of anything." He shook a finger in her face. "The sooner you get that into your pretty little head, the better off you'll be!"

"I don't believe it," Marlene said, echoing Reine's thoughts. "Cash was never a cruel boy."

Jasper turned on his wife. "He's a man, not a boy! He wants this land, and there's no saying what he'll do to get what he wants!"

"You mean, like his father?"

A current sizzled between husband and wife, making Reine back off.

"I'm not apologizing again for something that happened thirty-five years ago," her uncle said. "Everyone's entitled to a mistake."

"But what you did was not a mistake, Jasper," Marlene ground out. "And now you want to believe Cash is as calculating and cruel as you were."

The room screamed with the sudden silence that followed the accusation. Reine held her breath. Even though she'd known the truth for years, she shouldn't be here to witness this private agony.

"You've never forgiven me, have you, Marlene?"

"I've never forgotten. There's a difference."

"Bull. I see the truth in your eyes, woman, and hear it in your tone." Jasper shook his silver head in disgust. "If I'm such a monster, I don't know how you've managed to live with me all these years."

"Sometimes I don't know, either."

An expletive burst through Jasper's lips and he stormed out of the room.

Marlene burst into tears.

Reine rushed to her aunt's side, sat and put her arms around the woman who'd been a mother to her since her own had died more than twenty years before.

"Gray's all I have, all I ever really had...." As if suddenly aware of the niece holding her, Marlene quickly added, "Until you came along, of course."

Reine gave her shoulders a squeeze. "I know you love me, Aunt Marlene. And Uncle Jasper loves you."

Reine did believe that, even as she believed the gruff and sometimes-unkind man loved her, as well.

"Jasper tolerates me," her aunt said.

"He's an idiot to treat you like he does."

Reine wished she could say that he just didn't know any better, but she didn't believe it. Jasper Matlock was a crafty devil who knew exactly what he was doing at all times—and sometimes it seemed that he chose not to be human. Not that she would admit as much to her aunt.

Instead, she said, "Even an idiot knows a good thing when he sees her."

"Then why isn't he sitting here with me? Why aren't his arms around me instead of yours?"

Reine couldn't answer that any more than she could explain the way Cash had walked away from *her* so easily. To be fair, Cash had been forcibly pulled away, but that didn't mean he couldn't have come back for her.

"We should be going through this together," Marlene said. "Jasper should be thinking about Gray's safety."

"I'm sure he is."

"But he's more concerned with other things. I don't really think it's the money. It's that he's obsessing about Cash again."

"No more than Cash obsesses about him, I'm sure. It's Uncle Jasper's way of coping. He'd rather be angry than appear vulnerable."

"You believe that?"

"I do. Uncle Jasper loves Gray," she said.

"But what if something happens to Gray? What if it already has?"

"I'm sure it hasn't."

Though she was sure of no such thing, Reine was set on soothing her aunt.

Marlene rose and walked to the windows even as the sound of a car engine grew closer.

"Reine, someone's just arrived," she said softly as the engine was cut. "Sam Valdez. I wonder what he wants."

"I'll find out."

Reine headed for the front entrance and opened the door for the neighboring rancher.

Despite his Hispanic last name, Sam Valdez bore no resemblance to his father's ancestors. He appeared to be pure Anglo, with his blue eyes, short, rounded nose and dark red hair. Having reached middle age, he showed some gray at the temples and a little thicker waistline than she remembered, but he still appeared a man to be reckoned with. He was over six feet tall and more powerfully built than even Cash.

"Why, Reine," Valdez said, his pale eyes narrowing on her, "it's been a while."

"That it has, Mr. Valdez." She had the distinct

feeling that he wasn't exactly pleased to see her. "Can I help you?"

"I'm here to offer *my* help. I heard about Gray."

Wondering how far the word had spread, she said, "That's very kind of you, but I'm afraid this just isn't a good time for company."

Valdez moved around her, saying, "I'll only stay a few minutes." He approached her aunt, who still stood at the window, staring into the night. "Marlene, tell me what I can do for you."

"I wish I could say." Hands clasped in front of her as if she were holding herself together, Marlene turned to face the rancher. An odd light filled her eyes. And unshed tears. "To tell you the truth, Sam, I'm surprised you're here at all."

So was Reine. She didn't ever remember Uncle Jasper being friendly with him.

"We've been neighbors a lifetime." Valdez stepped forward to engulf Marlene's hands in his. "No matter our occasional differences, neighbors help one another in times of trouble. I believe I heard something about a kidnapper."

Marlene nodded. "It's so late. He still hasn't called back with the ransom demand." Freeing her hands, she began pacing and gave Reine a stricken expression. "Why not?"

"I don't know."

"Probably tryin' to make you nervous is all, Marlene. Make certain you come over with the goods. Is that where Jasper is, scraping up cash?"

"I—I don't know. And what if the man Jasper spoke to isn't a kidnapper at all?" she asked, sounding a bit desperate. "What if he's merely an opportunist who heard about Gray's being missing? He could have made that call, then gotten cold feet.''

''If that's true,'' Valdez said, ''then where is Gray?''

Her aunt swallowed hard. ''What if my son is...dead?''

''Now don't you go thinkin' like that, Marlene,'' Valdez said gruffly. ''Your boy'll turn up, you wait and see.''

Reine stared down at her thumb and imagined a tiny scar there. *All for one and one for all.* She would know if Gray was dead, wouldn't she? She wasn't ready to believe it.

''Nothing is going to happen to him,'' she said softly. ''We won't let it.''

''How will we stop it?'' asked her aunt.

''I don't know yet.''

That was why she'd gone to Cash. *He* would be able to figure it out, she was certain, if only he cared enough to try. Why didn't he? she wondered yet again.

''Maybe you ought to leave it to the menfolk,'' Valdez suggested none too subtly to Reine.

''That's what I have been doing, but so far, they've come up with nothing.''

''You're not thinkin' of bringing in the sheriff, are you?'' he asked intently. ''That could foul everything up, bring harm to your cousin.''

''No,'' Reine said, feeling a bit uncomfortable under his close scrutiny. ''No sheriff.''

''Then what *do* you intend to do?''

''Whatever I must.''

And obviously, she'd do it alone.

Cash's attitude still bitterly disappointed her. That

his own brother didn't seem to mean a thing to him broke Reine's heart all over again.

Friday

HAVING SLEPT LITTLE enough to put himself in a foul mood, Cash went in search of his Uncle Nemesio first thing the next morning. His mother's brother had taken him in when he'd been thrown off the Matlock spread. In addition to giving him a place to eat and sleep, Nemesio had made a man of him. He'd given him a man's strength, a hunger for justice, and a trade—the nearly lost art of building with real adobe.

Now the tables were turned and Nemesio Escobar worked for Cash Development. As Vice President of Traditional Construction, he had a fancy title, received a generous salary, and was expected to do little more than keep an eye on things.

Cash knew that fact grated on Nemesio, who hated being some "charity case," as he called it. Cash also knew that the older man chafed at not having done more with his own life, and he suspected Nemesio resented working for him at times. Yet, work he did. Hard.

Like his mother and old Ignacio, his uncle wouldn't sit around and take life easy. He insisted on working side by side with his men from start to finish.

Arriving at the site where they made their own mud bricks, Chase stepped down from his customized truck and strode past the front-end loader that was scooping up earth from nearly five feet below the surface. They couldn't dig deeper or they'd hit too much gravel.

"Mr. Abreu!" the driver yelled over the noise of his machinery. "Mornin'!"

"Hank. Where's my uncle?"

The driver pointed to the small, weathered structure that served as the supervisor's office.

Cash waved to the man and strode toward the shack, past the soil being dumped onto a vibrating screen where large stones were removed before it was deposited onto a conveyor belt.

Stabilizing adobe with cement was the newest technique used to keep the mud from washing away. While Cash appreciated the buildings constructed with traditional adobe and had a crew of men who still did restorations of the old structures, he was smart enough to realize that keeping up with the times for new projects was only good business.

He glanced at the nozzle injecting the soil with cement and watched the processed earth drop into a forklift scoop where another worker added water and straw, then drove the mixture to a metal form where he cast the actual bricks. They cured in the dry desert air for at least a week before being moved to the construction site.

The row upon row of stacked twelve-by-sixteen-inch mud bricks reflected the size of the new site—a strip mall going up at the edge of Santa Fe.

Drawing close to the ramshackle office, Cash heard what sounded like an argument drift through the open doorway. The clatter and clank of equipment made it impossible to hear more than bits and pieces. Still, he recognized a woman's voice. His mother's.

What in the world was she doing here?

"...need that kind of help!" he heard her shout.

Cash frowned. His mother rarely raised her voice and never with her older brother. If his uncle responded, he couldn't tell.

Consumed with curiosity, he picked up his pace, and upon reaching the office, filled the doorway.

Her back to him, hands on her hips, his mother faced down his uncle, who seemed trapped behind a messy desk. A traditional Pueblo shirt stretched over his barrel chest, his long, silver-streaked black hair held back from his ruddy round face by a bandanna, Nemesio Escobar didn't fit comfortably into an office setting of any kind.

And he obviously didn't care for whatever his sister had been saying to him. He might not be saying anything back, but he sure was glowering.

Stepping into the tension-filled room, Cash said, "Mom, you didn't say anything about coming out here today or I would have brought you myself."

His mother started, and when she turned to him, her expression seemed almost guilty—no doubt about the shouting, Cash figured.

"Son, I—I didn't expect to see you here, either."

"So what's up?"

"I promised Nemesio some of my homemade tamales next time I made them."

The delicious smell filled the small room. Cash eyed the covered basket that balanced precariously on a nearby file cabinet. It was large enough to hold a week's worth of food for a man. Undoubtedly, she'd brought enough for the whole crew to sample.

"Tamales for breakfast, huh?" he murmured.

"I have some things to do. I didn't think I'd find the time to swing by later," she said, sounding oddly defensive. "What about you? What are *you* doing here?"

"Just checking on things," Cash hedged.

Nemesio, on the other hand, was his usual blunt self. "Luna told me about Gray."

Grayson Matlock's disappearance was the very thing that had kept Cash up most of the night. Actually, he'd hoped to hash out his feelings over the matter with the uncle whose opinion he respected, but his mother's presence discouraged him from being open. He didn't want to involve her.

So, when his uncle asked, "What you gonna do about it?" Cash muttered, "Leave it to Matlock."

"Good."

"Nemesio!" Luna hissed. "This is Cash's blood you speak of."

"But not yours and not mine!"

"What does it matter who mothered him?"

"Whoa!" Cash said, wondering if this was what they'd been arguing over. "I don't want the two of you getting hot at each other for my sake."

Sister and brother gave each other conspiratorial looks that left him out of their loop.

"You see? Your son is being sensible," Nemesio said.

Cash spoke with more conviction than he was feeling: "Gray'll be all right."

"You can't know that," his mother mumbled.

No, he couldn't. It was the reason for his loss of sleep. But he didn't want to get involved. It was too complicated. Getting involved might interfere with his plans.

And yet...

What if something did happen to Gray while he stood around with his finger up his nose?

Unclenching his jaw, he asked, "What is it you want me to do, Mom?"

She seemed torn for a moment. Then, avoiding his gaze, she said, "I can't advise you."

His mother not having an opinion on something was enough to take Cash aback, especially after she'd been yelling about it. A small woman, she had big opinions. This wasn't like her, not at all. Then, again, she had good reason to want to stay out of this particular situation.

Better reason than he.

Even so, she softened for a moment, saying, "You'll have to follow your own heart."

Cash's laugh was humorless. "You're giving me credit for having one."

Her serious dark gaze met his. "I know my son better than anyone."

Indeed, she did. Cash grew instantly uncomfortable. Undoubtedly she was able to read his inner struggle without his ever saying a word.

Still, he protested, "Blood doesn't make us brothers."

Maybe if he said it often enough…

"You were brothers before you even knew the truth about Jasper. That will never change."

"Leave the boy alone!" Nemesio suddenly snapped as he shot to his feet.

Boy? Cash gaped.

Everyone was in a weird mood, as if they'd all been infected by some damned virus, he groused to himself. Here his uncle was working for him—a thirty-five-year-old man—and talking about him as if he were still a kid who needed his butt wiped.

"It is Cash's decision alone to make," Luna told her brother.

"Or not." Nemesio drew himself together. While he wasn't a tall man by anyone's standards, he radiated power—and, at the moment, a great deal of satisfaction. "Maybe things are working out the way they should, for once."

"Nemesio!"

"With Gray gone, Matlock has only one son. He'll have to recognize Cash at last."

"You speak as if Gray is dead," Luna said.

"Would that be so bad?"

She gasped.

Cash was equally shocked by his uncle's harsh words. Nemesio had hated Jasper Matlock with a passion since the truth had come out. Because Luna's pregnancy interfered with Matlock's plan to marry Marlene for the river property, he'd married his mistake off to his foreman. Luna hadn't fought it. Knowing Zane had been sweet on her, she'd chosen to give her unborn child a father who'd promised to love them both.

Nemesio had talked about getting even with Matlock for years, but as far as Cash knew, he'd never acted on the threat. His being protective of the people he loved, holding a grudge against anyone who hurt them, was only normal.

What bothered Cash was that Gray had never done anything to earn Nemesio's animosity. This was the heat of anger speaking, he assured himself. Anger and speculation. No more.

"I want nothing from Jasper Matlock save his

spread,'' Cash reminded them. "On *my* terms. Cold, hard cash.''

"Maybe now you'll get your hands on it," Nemesio muttered darkly as he headed for the door. "I got work to tend to.''

"I need to go, as well," Luna said. "Cash, you'll be home for supper?''

"I haven't decided what I'm going to do.''

Not about the evening meal, at least.

FROM HIS VANTAGE POINT in the barranca, Cash looked down from the barren hill to the spread that he'd vowed would be his someday.

He didn't give a damn about the century-old hacienda or the surrounding adobe buildings that were home to the household staff and ranch hands, horses and dogs. He didn't care about the cattle scattered over the more verdant valley and hillsides.

The land was what mattered.

Horses and cars, paintings and sculptures, buildings and shopping centers—he collected them all. The harder something was to get, the bigger the challenge, the more he wanted it. He was practically salivating over Matlock Ranch and would continue to do so until it was his.

Then, undoubtedly he'd be bored with it as he was with his numerous other holdings.

Life was a game and he was a player, but he wouldn't be a winner until he had all the pieces in his possession. A reporter had once asked him how much was enough. He'd said he'd give his answer when he got there.

But would he ever?

He'd spent the last decade making money and

spending it at a proportionately increasing rate. One would think he'd be happier.

Happy? What did that mean? He barely understood the concept anymore.

But as he studied the land, remembered laughter echoed in his mind. And a big splash of water. He cut his gaze well beyond the compound and imagined he could pin the spot where creek and river converged.

Twenty years ago...

He'd been fifteen, Gray fourteen, Reine twelve.

The rains had come with driving force, swelling the banks of every waterway in the valley. Tired of the long dry spell when rivers trickled down to creek-size and creeks dried up altogether, they'd ridden out to see. He and Gray had dared Reine to shed her clothing and skinny-dip just to make her blush. They wouldn't actually have gone through with it, her being a kid and all. But she'd gotten her dander up, had told them off and had pushed Gray into the water.

Gray had looked so comical when he'd come up for air that Cash couldn't help but laugh. He'd been so busy making fun of his best buddy that he'd never seen it coming—his turn into the drink. Shy little Reine had gotten them both. Then it had been her turn to laugh.

They'd all laughed.

They'd all been happy.

He'd been happy then.

REINE DECIDED A RIDE would serve double duty, beginning with clearing her mind. She'd slept only in fits and starts and she was feeling a little loose around the edges.

Unsettled. Unfocused.

She saddled up Gold Mine, a Palomino her aunt had bought for her some dozen years before—as if she'd needed a lure to get Reine to drive the half hour from Santa Fe to the ranch....

The Matlocks had taken Reine in when her mother, Marlene's younger sister, had died in a freak drowning accident. Her father had skipped out on them years before, when her mother had stopped giving him access to her trust fund. He'd been a charmer, her mother had always said, but he'd also been a cheat. Reine couldn't even remember what Laurence Kendrick looked like—she'd ripped up the photos her mother had kept of him. Nor did she care.

As far as she was concerned, Marlene, Jasper and Gray were the only family she needed....

Poor Aunt Marlene had been up and pacing all night. She'd been awake forty-eight hours straight. Exhaustion and stress had finally claimed her around dawn.

Thankful that she wouldn't have to worry about the heartsick woman for a while, Reine figured she would take this opportunity to get a lead on her cousin's kidnapper.

That meant finding Tobiah Hill—her second purpose in taking out Gold Mine.

The foreman of Matlock Ranch was here with his men, rounding up and moving cattle—an undertaking that had been interrupted by Gray's disappearance. Yesterday, nothing had been done on the spread unless it had been absolutely necessary. Gray had been everyone's focus. The search parties had come up with nothing, however, and Uncle Jasper had reluctantly sent his ranch hands back to work first thing this morning.

Reine knew they would put in a long day, and she couldn't wait until supper to get started.

Who knew how long Gray had before something unthinkable happened to him? The longer he was gone, the more likely that would be.

Why couldn't Cash have shown some concern? she wondered. How could he be so cold? As boys, he and Gray had been inseparable, and not from Uncle Jasper's lack of trying. How many times had the man warned Gray to stay away from the hired help's ''whelp''?

She shook her head sadly. Uncle Jasper could be so cruel. He'd known Cash was his natural son all along, and he'd treated him as if he were worthless.

And look how Cash had fooled him.

Reine figured Cash could do anything he set his mind to. He'd proved that, day in and day out. His wealth far exceeded her uncle's and Jasper Matlock wasn't a poor man, by any means. Why couldn't Cash have set his mind to repairing the chasm between them? Instead, he'd chosen to compete.

He was wealthier.

More ruthless.

Greedier.

He was not a man she could like. But she didn't need Cash, Reine told herself. She'd done without him for seventeen years and she could do without him for another seventy.

Besides, she had Tobiah Hill.

Nothing went on around Matlock Ranch that the foreman didn't know about. She meant to question him thoroughly. He was a quiet one, but he didn't miss a thing. He'd be able to name every person who had it in for Jasper.

Or for Gray, for that matter, though she really didn't want to think it possible. Everyone liked her cousin, she reminded herself. He didn't have enemies—none she knew of, anyway.

If only she could believe that Gray's disappearance was simply about money....

This *had* to be about something more, or the kidnapper would have put a price on Gray's head from the first. Whoever had taken her cousin wanted Uncle Jasper to suffer. The sins of the father were being visited on the son.

How unfair.

Reine was considering how cruel life could be when Gold Mine snorted and threw up her head as if in greeting to another horse. Reine heard hoofbeats coming up rapidly behind them.

''Whoa,'' she murmured, slowing and turning in the saddle for a look.

Expecting to see one of the ranch hands heading out from the compound, she was startled by the familiar figure riding an Appaloosa straight at her, hell-bent for leather.

Cash!

Her pulse raced and her stomach knotted the second she recognized him. She only hoped Uncle Jasper was nowhere around, or there would be more trouble.

What was Cash doing on Matlock land?

Chapter Three

Cash slowed Akando as he caught up with Reine. Rather than bringing the horse to a full stop, he let him dance around the mare and show off some.

"Are you crazy?" were the first words out of Reine's mouth.

"Could be," he agreed.

"If Uncle Jasper catches you—"

"He'll what?" It took all his resources to keep his expression neutral. "Beat me and throw me off his land? Oh, that's right—he already did that. And his trying it again is highly unlikely. I've learned a thing or two about taking care of myself over the years."

"Don't even joke about it, Cash."

"I never joke."

Her blue eyes were inexplicably sad when her gaze meshed with his. "Did he beat that out of you, too?"

Too? Wondering what she meant by that, Cash wouldn't dwell on it. Instead, he concentrated on her.

This was more like it. When she'd come to his place, Reine had been buttoned-up, almost prim. Beautiful, yes, but as if all the life had been sucked out of her in comparison to the way she looked now.

Wearing jeans and a butter-cream shirt open at the

throat, her face free of makeup, her long hair swept up into a ponytail and tied with a yellow ribbon, she reminded him of the spirited girl he used to know.

Well...not quite.

Her features had matured. As had her breasts, he thought appreciatively, biting back a smile. She'd finally gotten some. He remembered that had been her main concern at fifteen.

"Thought you'd be with your aunt."

"She's finally getting some rest," Reine said tersely. "Do you ride this way often?"

"Often enough."

Her expression was disapproving. Maybe she'd changed more than he'd thought. A wave of regret swept through Chase, and he wondered if she would go straight to Matlock with the information.

Suddenly she said, "You don't scare me, you know."

Cash started. "I didn't know I was trying."

"You did yesterday."

"Scared you?"

"You tried to."

When he gave her a challenging expression, her cheeks flushed the way he knew they would. The way they had the day before. The way they had all those years ago. She'd always flustered easily. He'd always enjoyed the fact.

That hadn't changed.

"So, are you going to tell me what you want or what?" she demanded.

Not ready to make any concessions, he kept stringing her along. "What if I said, 'You.'"

Her deepening color pleased him more than all of

his possessions lumped together—maybe because it was so elusive, something he couldn't buy.

"Could I have you?" he asked softly and only half in jest.

"Dream on, Cash."

He shrugged. "Don't have dreams anymore. Just bank accounts."

Again, her eyes were sad. "Poor you," she murmured.

His laugh was humorless. "Not exactly."

"Yes, Cash," she insisted. "Exactly."

Without warning, she started off. Ticked at her attempt at pity, he reined Akando in close and paced her. She cut alongside a pasture where cattle grazed peacefully.

Who was she to make judgments on his life choices? Reine Kendrick had always had everything she'd ever wanted. Her mother, aunt and trust fund had all seen to that.

He rode in silence, following her lead. She took him through a patchwork of fields, edged with willows and cottonwood where the acequias cut through, bringing much-needed water to the entire spread.

"So where are you headed?" he finally asked.

"Where you don't want to go."

"How can you be sure of that?"

She arched her brows and asked, "Have you changed your mind, then?"

"About what?"

"Gray. Why else would you be on Matlock land?"

He wasn't ready to make any admissions that would give her the upper hand. "Maybe I'm just taking stock of what'll be mine soon."

"Lusting after what you can't have?"

"Everything has its price."

"What's yours?" she asked.

"Mine?" He frowned at her. "I don't get it."

"For helping me find Gray before it's too late. What would it cost me?"

His gut clenched. *Too late?* Surely not. Though she continued to keep her tone light, he caught a glimpse of anguish in her gaze.

Cash realized they'd reached the creek near the old chile mill. Reine picked her way around the rocks and boulders and along the trickling stream. She was headed straight for the box canyon and their youthful haunt. He hadn't been here in decades, but he remembered every inch of the way.

From the stream, they followed the ditch that once fed the water to the mill. They rounded a bend and there it was. The foundation posts appeared precarious, yet what was left of the weather-beaten building still managed to stay upright.

The abandoned gristmill had made a perfect "clubhouse" for him and Gray when Matlock had discouraged an open friendship. And later, for Reine, too, after they'd allowed her into their secret society.

Cash wondered how much she remembered about the place where Jasper Matlock had found them together that one time they'd made love.

He decided to keep his own counsel on that matter.

Reine dismounted and led the Palomino to a struggling cottonwood, where she flung her reins over a low branch. Cash followed suit.

Only then did he ask, "What have you learned so far?"

"Nothing yet."

"What about the kidnapper?"

"We haven't heard from him again." She shook her head. "And that really scares me."

"But you believe Gray's alive."

"Yes," she agreed. "And I want him to stay that way."

Her certainty gave him some measure of relief. The three of them had been closer than true siblings by the very nature of their proscribed friendship. Surely one of them would sense it if Gray was dead.

"So what's your price, Cash?" she asked again.

"I have everything I could possibly want—"

"Do you really?"

Her gaze was measuring, making him shift inside. *He didn't have her.*

Was that what she was offering?

Tension radiated between them as it had the day before, and not only because she'd come to ask help for a Matlock. She looked at him as a woman looked at a man she was attracted to. That little show he'd put on for her benefit yesterday hadn't disgusted her quite as much as she'd wanted him to believe.

"Well, there is one thing I don't have," he admitted.

"Which is?"

Cash hesitated for only a second before saying, "This spread." He couldn't quite bring himself to open old wounds.

"The land's not mine to offer."

"Then what *are* you suggesting?"

He was close enough to see the way her eyes changed—her attempt at veiling her thoughts from him. *All right, then. Let* her *be the one to bring it up.*

"How about...a big donation to your favorite charity?"

He should have known she wouldn't have the guts to give voice to her real thoughts.

"Sounds good," he said smoothly. "By the way, my favorite charity is me."

She rolled her eyes. "You haven't changed. You're *still* impossible."

"Not impossible. A challenge." One he wanted her to take. Why not?

She'd grown into a very desirable woman. He'd spent years forgetting her. Years building his fortune. Years attending social events to which he'd brought companions who reminded him of her. All had been blond, beautiful, smart.

But none had been Reine.

This bit of game playing—maybe this was her way of approaching him. Maybe she *was* offering herself as payment. Subtly, of course.

Why else would she have brought him *here,* of all places?

GRAY STRUGGLED AGAINST the haze that held him captive every bit as much as the ropes binding his hands and feet together. They must have drugged the food he'd been spoon-fed. He couldn't do for himself, not trussed up like a heifer. They'd dumped him here on a bedroll and left....

How long ago?

He'd lost all track of time.

"Why don't you just admit it?"

He heard the voice from afar. A woman's.

"You're as worried about Gray as the rest of us,"

she was saying. *"Admit he's the reason you're here."*

That was *Reine's* voice.

She was talking about him to someone. They must be searching for him, then. He tried calling out to her, but tape over his mouth prevented him from doing more than making some unintelligible sounds.

"If that'll make you happy," came a familiar male voice, *"go ahead and believe whatever you want."*

Gray made a concerted effort to move himself so he could see outside. He managed to work himself into a sitting position. Managed to focus long enough to get a glimpse out the window.

Cash!

He knew he'd recognized the voice.

Cash and Reine had come back to their hideaway to find him. He tried harder to call out, but only succeeded in making low, garbled sounds.

And then it was too late.

He saw them move toward their horses.

In his mind, he shouted, *Wait! I'm inside!*

But of course they couldn't hear his muffled plea. They would leave and he would be alone once more. Not that it was likely he'd be alone for long. Surely one of the men would be back to check on him any time now. Then, who knew what would happen?

Desperate, Gray fell to his side and rolled. Then he wriggled until his feet were aimed at the wall. Lying on his back, he pulled up his knees and struck out as hard as he could. His boots went right through the rotting wall without making much noise. He angled himself and aimed at another spot. It was just as weak. Even a third effort—this one more solid, the results louder—brought no response.

Obviously, no one heard.

His energy depleted for the moment, Gray settled back to wait.

And to plot his escape.

WITH AN UNEASY TRUCE between Cash and her, Reine retraced her path toward the mouth of the canyon on foot, meaning to water the horses at the creek before they remounted. But when the hairs on the back of her neck prickled, she stopped and glanced back at the abandoned mill.

"Did you hear something?"

Cash turned, too, his gaze seeming to pierce every inch of the small canyon.

"Must be a coyote or rabbit," he finally said.

"No...well...maybe."

She listened hard but heard nothing more. Her imagination was getting the best of her.

They moved on to the creek and let the horses drink.

She'd detoured Cash to the old mill purposely. She'd hoped the place could do what she hadn't been able to manage. But if sentiment could affect him, he wasn't showing it. He wouldn't admit to anything but wanting to fulfill his vow to Jasper Matlock.

For a moment, she'd been certain he was going to say something else—something about her.

If he had... Reine wasn't actually certain what she would have done.

Cash had changed so much—his attitude toward life, his self-involvement, his polished good looks.

His clothes all carried designer labels, she was certain. His boots were definitely handmade. His once-tangled black hair was now cut short and crisp. His strong features—aquiline nose, high forehead, square chin—were bronzed just enough to set off green sparks in his hazel eyes.

Gone were all traces of the wild boy she'd given her heart to. This man was controlled.

And controlling, Reine reminded herself.

"I wonder if they've heard anything from the kidnapper yet," she murmured, broaching the subject yet again.

"You didn't say what the law was doing to find Gray in the meantime."

"No law. Uncle Jasper wouldn't hear of it. I think that's a mistake, but he's afraid for Gray's life if he goes against the kidnapper's orders."

"That's what the bastard is counting on. *You* could bring in the sheriff."

"No. I won't defy him."

"So that hasn't changed, either," Cash muttered, vaulting himself into the saddle.

Unable to think of an appropriate response in her defense, Reine followed suit and headed for the section of the range where she expected to find Tobiah Hill.

A LOUD RINGING STARTLED Jasper straight up in his chair.

Having drifted off while going over his personal finances, he was instantly awake.

The phone rang again.

He wrapped a trembling hand around the receiver and lifted it to his ear.

"Matlock, here."

"Mr. Matlock," said the sexless voice he'd been hoping to hear. "Are you ready to do business?"

"What have you done with my son?" Jasper demanded.

A chilly laugh from the other end scraped up his spine.

"If you're not going to be serious, we have nothing to discuss."

"Please! I just want to be sure Gray is all right."

He sweated out the silence, fearing the caller would hang up. But the connection remained viable.

Finally, the kidnapper said, "Gray is alive and well...for the moment. Whether or not he stays in good health all depends on your willingness to cooperate."

Of course, he'd do anything in his power to assure Gray's safety. Realizing that this was one situation where his demands would get him nowhere, Jasper got a grip on himself.

"What is it you want from me?"

"First...assurance there won't be any interference from the authorities—"

"I didn't call them! I won't!"

"Good. Second...the reward for Gray's being returned in one piece."

Jasper saw red on that one. "Reward"—his Aunt Fanny! This was extortion!

He tried not to sound too anxious when he asked, "How much?"

"Two million."

He closed his eyes. Where the hell was he going to get two million dollars? Having just gone over his books, he figured the most he could easily get his hands on by cashing in all his and Marlene's personal investments was a little over three hundred thousand.

"I don't have access to that kind of cash."

"Then I suggest you get it. Fast."

"How?" He couldn't help sounding desperate.

"You have assets," the icy voice reminded him. "Surely you have *something* of value to sell. I'll give you until sundown on Monday."

"Three days? That's impossible!"

"It better be possible or you won't see your son again…alive. Until Monday…"

"Wait!"

But the line went dead.

Jasper sat, stunned, unable to move.

Two million…in cash…three days.

What the hell was he going to do?

Sell "something of value," as the kidnapper had instructed?

Matlock Construction was already in big trouble. Few people other than himself knew how big.

But the ranch was unencumbered by debt. He'd made sure of that. And it was worth a heck of lot more than two million, though for a quick sale he'd probably have to settle for a lot less than its true worth.

What a nightmare!

If he wanted to see Gray alive, he'd have to sell off most if not all of Matlock Ranch. And he could only think of one man who both wanted the property and would be able to come up with that kind of money fast.

The name came to him again like a curse—*Cash!*

Was this the bastard's newest plan to get his hands on the spread?

At Zane Abreu's funeral, Cash had vowed that he'd take everything Jasper cared about from him. Jasper had figured Cash would forget about the empty threat once he'd cooled down. And it had seemed as if he had.

But Cash had merely been biding his time.

Jasper wasn't blind, deaf and dumb. He knew the financial problems at Matlock Construction had been orchestrated by the whelp. If he lost the company, he would know whom to blame.

And if he lost the ranch...or Gray lost his life? *Would that be Cash's doing, as well?*

Chapter Four

Cash remembered Tobiah Hill as the kind of man who, because he said little, heard more than most. Therefore, Reine's idea about seeking out the foreman for information that might give them a lead made sense.

Not that he'd actually committed himself to anything. He was merely going along for the ride.

"Matlock know you're playing detective?" Cash asked, wondering what Reine meant to do with whatever she learned.

"I didn't say anything, no."

"Why not? You'd think he'd be grateful. But that's not his style, is it?"

"Uncle Jasper can be a difficult man...."

Difficult was too kind a word as far as he was concerned.

"Sort of like you," Reine added, raising his hackles.

"Don't compare me to that bastard!"

"'That bastard' happens to be your father."

"My father is dead and buried."

Zane Abreu would always be his real father, Cash thought, no matter the accident of his birth.

"And how do you think Zane would feel about what you've become?"

Not missing the disapproval in her tone, he said, "He'd be proud I made something of my life."

"Really?"

Before he could demand that she explain herself, Reine urged her Palomino into a lope and shot ahead.

Akando was revving for a match race, but Cash kept him—and his own temper—under control. *Let her have the lead—for now.*

It wasn't long before the occasional stray cow multiplied until they were cutting through a herd toward hired hands who were conferring at the far end of the pasture. A couple of the boys rode off while a few others hung around the truck that was being used as a chuck wagon.

When they rode up, the foreman was just pouring himself a cup of coffee and having a face-down with one of his men. Cash recognized the bald man with skin tanned as dark as old leather. Ozzie Skinner was a local man who'd drifted in and out of the valley ever since he could remember.

Grasping his brimmed hat in one hand, lit cigar in the other, the hired hand said smoothly, "I'm tellin' you, I couldn't get here no sooner this mornin'."

"This is your last warning, Skinner," the foreman replied. "No more of this showing up when it suits you."

Reine and Cash dismounted and tied up their horses at a hitching post that had been set up near the truck, where they hung back to wait until Tobiah was free.

"Then give me a coupla days off officially," Skinner was saying, his tone wheedling. "That'd be best. I pulled something in my back the other day and sittin' in this saddle ain't makin' it feel none too good, I can tell you. I could hardly move this mornin', no less roll outta my bunk."

"Take all the days you need," Tobiah agreed, "long as you don't mind finding yourself another place when you decide your back is better."

"Are you sayin' you don't believe me?"

"Don't matter whether I do or not. I'm not running this operation shorthanded. There's at least a dozen outta-work men around town who'll be glad to take your place if you don't need it. Now back to work."

Cash didn't miss the sour expression that crossed Skinner's homely face before he stuffed his cigar into his mouth, mumbled, "Yessir!" and stomped off toward his horse.

Tobiah took a long swig of coffee and grumbled, "Slacker."

Reine poked Cash in the side and moved toward the foreman.

Cash hadn't seen the man since his daddy's funeral seventeen years before. Then, Tobiah had just been one of the dozens of young cowboys on the Matlock spread, and so Cash was a little startled when they came face-to-face. Tobiah couldn't be much older than his mother, but hard outdoor work had left its stamp on his sun-wrinkled face, thin whipcord-hard body and grizzled hair and mustache.

"Miss Reine," the foreman said, though he wasn't actually looking at her.

His pale blue eyes had gone all spooky when

they'd settled on Cash. Not knowing what Tobiah might be thinking about his presence, Cash kept his expression neutral and nodded in a friendly manner.

"Tobiah. Been a long time."

"That it has, Cash. Truth to tell, I'm surprised to see you here."

"Makes two of us."

"Tobiah," Reine said, finally getting the man's full attention. "I was hoping you could spare a few minutes to talk to me."

"About Gray? Nothing new to tell you, miss. Sorry. We lost his trail and couldn't pick it up again."

"I meant about who might be responsible for his disappearance in the first place."

"Wouldn't know nothing about that."

"You might be surprised at how much more you know than you realize," she assured him, her manner more charming than any Chase had seen to date. "So, will you talk to me?"

"Course I'll help you any way I can." He returned his spooky gaze to Cash. "So why're *you* here?"

Reine joined in, challenging him with a look, as well. Cash felt as if he'd been put on the spot. Unfortunately, he couldn't get around the foreman the way he could her.

"Let's say I don't want anything to happen to Gray that could be prevented."

Tobiah nodded with seeming satisfaction, but Reine couldn't quite hide her frustration. Cash smiled inside but remained outwardly passive.

The foreman refilled his cup, saying, "Help yourself to some coffee."

"Don't mind if I do," Cash said. "Reine?"

"None for me, thanks."

Cash quickly filled a tin cup, then followed them around the chuck wagon.

"Think I'll take a load off," Tobiah was saying.

Indicating the logs set into an incline that could be used as crude benches, the foreman sat himself down on one. When Cash joined Reine on the other, he couldn't miss her discomfort at the near contact. Cash saluted her with his cup and took a slug of coffee. She inched over, putting as much distance between them as possible.

"Now, what exactly can I tell you, Miss Reine?" Tobiah asked.

"Well, I was trying to figure out why anyone would want to kidnap Gray in the first place—"

"Greed, pure and simple."

"I'm not so sure there's anything simple about it," she argued. "I wonder if someone doesn't have a vendetta against my uncle."

"Yep, 'someone' sure does." His gaze flashed meaningfully to Cash.

"True." No point in Cash denying it when Tobiah Hill had been at his daddy's funeral and had witnessed his showdown with Matlock. "But I had nothing to do with this. I would never put an innocent person in jeopardy." He didn't add *especially not Gray.* "You can't tell me I'm the only one who has something against Matlock."

"Didn't say that. But you're the most likely who's willing and able to do something about it."

Cash felt his temper rise at what was practically an accusation. "The old man's been bad-mouthing me again?"

"Let's not go there," Reine interjected, placing a hand on his arm.

He couldn't resist her pleading expression. He could lose himself in her beautiful blue eyes—not to mention the rest of her. Trying to ignore the effect of her touch, he took a quick sip of coffee and told himself to simmer down.

"Who else has it in for Uncle Jasper?"

The foreman slowly shook his head.

"You haven't heard any threats?" she asked. "Or witnessed any arguments?"

The grizzled head suddenly stilled and a thoughtful expression crossed his features. He started to say something, then backed down, mumbling, "Naw, nothing."

"Let us decide that," Cash said.

"Didn't have to do with the ranch, as I can tell."

It was Reine's turn. "What didn't?"

Tobiah shifted on the log. "This was a coupla weeks ago in Santa Fe. Mr. Matlock and me, we went our separate ways and agreed to meet back at the truck. He got there first, only he weren't alone."

"He was with a woman?" Cash guessed. Why else would the man seem so reluctant to say anything?

"Was he?" Reine asked.

Tobiah sighed. "A real looker. Early fifties, maybe. Dark hair with red fire in it."

"So they were arguing?"

When Tobiah did nothing more than nod, Cash wished he could pull the story out of the man.

"What were they arguing about?" Reine asked.

She was sounding as exasperated as he was beginning to feel.

"Couldn't hear, but..." The foreman hesitated again as if reluctant to go into it. He finally said, "I seen her slap him and run off into a nearby store."

"And you didn't ask him about it?"

"No, ma'am. He muttered something about Selena having foolish notions about life for a woman her age and then changed the subject."

"'Selena,'" Reine echoed thoughtfully. "Did Uncle Jasper mention her last name?"

"Nope."

Cash went back a few exchanges. "The store— which one was it?"

"Couldn't tell you exactly," Tobiah said with a shrug. "But it's one of them tourist galleries. Masks and kachinas in the window...and a real fancy set of pottery containers that look like pueblo buildings."

"Where is this?"

"On San Francisco, down from the plaza a bit."

He tried to visualize the shop. The Cash Development offices were located within Santa Fe proper, and while he spent as little time there as possible— the electronic age made working from his home office just as efficient and far more convenient—he was as familiar with the town as anyone. He was certain he knew the gallery.

"Uncle Jasper didn't say anything else about this Selena woman? No hint of what they were arguing over?"

"Afraid not."

And, unfortunately, the foreman didn't seem to be one to pry, Cash thought, wondering if this was a dead end. A lovers' quarrel.

Matlock was probably no more faithful to his wife than he'd been to Cash's mother.

"How about other disputes," he asked, "having to do with the business?"

"You'd know more about that than me," Tobiah returned pointedly. "My interest stays right here."

Reine jumped on that. "What about the spread? Any feuds with neighboring ranchers?"

"Only the usual arguments over water rights, Sam Valdez being the loudest mouth of the bunch."

Before Reine could pump the foreman for more details, Tobiah stood and waved a greeting to an oncoming horseman.

"Any more questions, maybe you'd better ask Mr. Matlock himself."

The owner of Matlock Ranch rode up to them, raising a cloud of red dust.

Cash's insides clutched as he stood and stared at the rider. Despite the fact that he'd voluntarily come into forbidden territory, he hadn't counted on running into the old man—an unpleasant surprise at best.

Matlock dismounted and quickly took in the small gathering. His gaze locked with Cash's for what seemed like an endless moment. Emotions rode over his features, leaving them in a glower.

Cash suspected he wasn't going to like what was coming.

Reine moved forward, asking, "Uncle Jasper, did you hear from the kidnappers?"

But the man ignored her, confirming Cash's worst suspicions when the first thing out of his mouth was, "What're you doing on my land?"

"Uncle Jasper—"

"Am I talking to you, girl?" His green eyes were cold and flat as he glared at Reine. "You mind your own business like I told you before."

"And like *I* said," she calmly told him, "Gray *is* my business."

Ignoring her again, he went straight for Cash. "I was right from the first. You're in the thick of it—the plan to get my spread."

His inability to deny this kept Cash from responding.

Even so, Matlock grabbed a fistful of his shirtfront. "What did you do with my boy?"

Cash held himself in check so he wouldn't respond in kind, but he was unable to hide his bitterness when he said, "You mean Gray?"

"I only have one son. You couldn't accept that." He jerked the material, pulling Cash closer. "You been doing your best to ruin me, but even I didn't pin you for the lowlife you are!"

"Uncle Jasper, please!"

It took all Cash's will not to strike out. He clenched his hands into fists but kept them at his sides.

His heart was pumping so hard he could barely hear Tobiah mutter, "Maybe we all better calm down here."

"Get your hands off me," Cash growled.

"Or you'll what? You aren't man enough to take me on face-to-face!" Matlock shouted, his own face redder than the New Mexican soil. "You go behind my back like some stinking yellow-belly, stealing bits of my company, ruining it a piece at a time, putting Matlock Construction in so deep a hole—"

"Which is called 'business.'"

Matlock tightened his grip so they were practically nose to nose. *"Business!"* he spat. "I guess you expect me to believe your going after my spread is just business, too?''

They were so close that Cash could feel Matlock's hot breath on his face. The perverse embrace reminded him of the only other time they'd had such intimate physical contact—when Matlock had caught him with Reine. Cash hadn't fought back then either. Part of him had figured he'd had it coming. Reine had only been fifteen. Still, he'd disliked Matlock from that day forward—and that had been nearly a year before learning the truth of his parentage.

Then, he'd learned to hate the man.

Feeling the flush of raw emotion anew, Cash spoke through clenched teeth. ''I'm warning you for the last time—let go!''

But Matlock was obviously beyond warnings.

''And because you haven't figured out a way to get my land on the up-and-up,'' he said, ''you act like the dog you are and take your sickness out on my boy!''

Finally, Cash lost it. Quick as lightning, he broke the man's grip on him and threw him to the ground, pinning him there, knees to his chest, one hand around the old buzzard's throat.

''Cash!'' Reine shouted.

Ignoring her protest as well as her ineffectual tugs at his shoulder, Cash tightened his grip enough to get Matlock's full attention.

''Now you listen to me, old man. I don't know what happened to Gray, but I intend to find out. Don't try to interfere with me. And if I were you, I wouldn't be making any more accusations against me, either. I would see you dead before harming one hair on Gray's head!''

Jasper Matlock's face was practically purple with rage when Cash finally moved off him and got to his feet. Reine raced to help her uncle up, with Tobiah right behind her, but when they grasped Jasper's arms, he pushed them aside and rose on his own, gasping.

Cash braced himself for a counterattack that didn't come.

Without another word, Matlock stormed past them all, launched himself into the saddle and rode off.

A choked sound got his attention. Reine. Her expression was accusing.

"How could you?" she demanded.

"How could I what?" he asked coldly. "Defend myself? I learned from the last time Matlock got rough with me, Reine—or is your memory so short?"

"God help me, I remember everything! I only wish I didn't!"

She shoved by him, her shoulder glancing off his upper arm, spinning him around. He watched her spring up into the saddle and ride off after the uncle she obviously cared more for than she did him.

"Do you think we'll ever see him again?" Marlene asked.

"Uncle Jasper?" He'd beaten Reine back to the house, had left his mount with one of the hands and had taken off again for parts unknown, this time in one of his four-wheel-drive vehicles. "Of course, we will."

"Not him."

Reine stopped folding linen napkins—they were

engaged in busywork meant to keep them both sane—and took her aunt's hands.

"Gray is alive, Aunt Marlene. You have to believe that."

"You're right, of course."

So why didn't the kidnapper call?

When she'd seen how agitated her uncle had been as he'd ridden toward them, she'd thought he'd received new information, and that they might finally have a way to move forward. Her aunt had dashed that hope. Uncle Jasper surely would have told *her* if he'd heard anything.

Marlene patted Reine's hand and pulled away. Picking up the tablecloth she'd just folded, she placed it carefully in the buffet drawer.

"Why did Jasper leave the ranch?" she asked.

Reine had been hoping to avoid the subject, but she saw that was impossible if she didn't want to worry her aunt further.

"He's pretty upset. Cash was here, on the range with me, talking to Tobiah Hill. I thought maybe your foreman could tell us something we didn't already know." Of course, her uncle's argument with a beautiful woman wasn't something Reine was ready to share. "Anyway, Uncle Jasper found us and lost his temper the moment he set eyes on Cash."

Marlene whipped around, looking distressed. "Oh, dear, is he all right?"

"Cash didn't hurt him."

"I meant *Cash*. This can't be easy for him, with his loyalties torn the way they've been."

"He's a man, as Uncle Jasper keeps saying. He can take care of himself."

"It may seem so on the outside. But he is human."

Marlene grasped the back of the formal dining chair and shook her head sadly. "I begged Jasper to make it right with him so many times over the years, but he never would."

Reine gave her aunt credit for not hating Cash herself. Marlene had always been sympathetic toward him, and even more so since learning that he was her husband's natural son—a child that Jasper had never wanted nor cared for. That Cash had tried to run Matlock Construction out of business didn't seem to change her feelings on the subject.

"Maybe Cash wouldn't have let him get close."

"He is a lot like Jasper, isn't he?" Marlene mused, echoing Reine's own thoughts. "I only wish Gray were more like his father."

Reine started. "You do?"

"A *little* more," she amended. "He's like me. Too open. Too forgiving. Too weak."

"Aunt Marlene, Gray is not weak. And you're the strongest woman I've ever met!" Reine insisted. "You'd have to be, considering the man you chose to marry."

"I didn't, you know," Marlene was quick to say. "Choose Jasper, that is. Papa did."

"Your father picked out your husband?"

Reine had never met the autocratic grandfather who'd died shortly after she'd been born. Reine's mother had left New Mexico to escape him, but she'd never shared this particular story with her daughter.

"Papa said I needed a strong man, one who was ambitious and attached to the land. He didn't want me marrying someone who would sell off my inheritance the moment he died."

Which, unfortunately, Reine's own father had

done to her mother to some extent by wasting whatever part of her trust fund he could get his hands on.

Marlene was saying, "Julio Valdez would have found some way to snap up the land in a heartbeat. He always claimed it should have been his in the first place, and he was tired of having to negotiate for water rights."

Reine knew the marriage had not only doubled her uncle's acreage but had given him direct access to the river, as well.

"Surely Grandfather could have made some legal arrangements to protect your heritage."

"He did, but that's not all he wanted. Papa liked to manage things, especially lives. He admired that trait in Jasper. Papa was right about him and the land, too," Aunt Marlene continued. "Jasper wouldn't think of selling off one foot of it. Not for anything. He did an awful thing to get what he wanted and he's not about to let go. It's always been the most important thing in his life."

"After you and Gray."

"It's the most important," Marlene insisted.

Reine didn't argue.

She feared that her aunt might be right.

REINE WAS RELIEVED WHEN her uncle returned home in time for dinner. Not that she had an appetite. Too keyed-up, she just couldn't sit around and wait any longer, but she hadn't wanted to leave her aunt alone.

Now she wouldn't have to.

After making certain Marlene had dinner preparations under control, she said, "I'm driving back to Santa Fe."

"When?"

"Actually, right now."

"Oh…" Unable to hide her disappointment, Marlene adopted a determined smile. "I suppose you have things you need to do."

"A few."

Like checking out that gallery and finding the mysterious Selena.

"But I'll be back sometime tomorrow," Reine promised. "In the meantime, if you hear anything—"

"I'll call."

She kissed her aunt goodbye and considered looking in on her uncle before leaving. His office door was closed, however, shutting her out as surely as the man himself would. He hadn't said a word to her since his return.

Let him be angry. *She* was angry. With him. With Cash.

Cash…

The vision of him pinning her uncle to the ground and appearing ready to strangle the life out of the man stayed with her all the way to her car.

Then, so had what he'd said—that he was going to find Gray.

How?

He knew nothing more than she…or did he?

She wondered if it had been an empty promise—words uttered in the heat of anger.

Reine remembered another embittered oath Cash had made at his daddy's funeral. For years, now, he'd been doing his best to fulfill that one. So would he be any less serious now?

Too bad he hadn't agreed to help her in the first place.

Reine only hoped she wasn't fooling herself in believing it was possible to save her cousin from some unknown fate. Gray had played a pivotal role in both their lives. Contrary to what he'd let her believe when she'd gone to ask him for his help, Cash had never forgotten. He'd merely been protecting himself by pretending Gray didn't matter.

Now they were both alone—each too stubborn to seek out the help of the other.

Chapter Five

Friday evening

That evening, Cash didn't know how long he sat across from the *trazo* where Reine made her home before making up his mind to leave his car and go in after her.

The small buildings with common walls and courtyards formed a continuous facade along the narrow side street in the old town. He opened the antique mesquite door that allowed him into a garden area whose fragrance immediately surrounded him, reminding him of Reine.

The sun was down, but it was still light enough to make out the wild display of poppies and asters, black-eyed Susans and buffalo berry. The courtyard was bursting with flora, including a large aspen tree alongside the wall. A brick pathway took him past a burbling fountain, cast-iron table and chairs, and terra-cotta planters filled with geraniums and assylium, straight up to the red brick single-story house.

Reine answered the door herself as he'd expected. Her surprise was evident in the way she stiffened and curled rose-tipped fingers around the wooden panel. Undoubtedly, she wasn't eager to see him again.

"What are you doing here?"

"Looking for a Friday-night date."

He slid his gaze over her. She'd switched to the restrained-if-feminine apparel she apparently preferred when not on horseback—a broomstick skirt and shirt buttoned up to the throat. The reserved attire made him yearn to explore the recklessness in her that he knew the clothing hid.

"You'll do," he murmured.

"What makes you believe I'd go anywhere with you?" she asked coolly.

Belying her tone, her color was rising to match the deep rose of her silk outfit.

"I thought you might be interested in checking out a certain gallery."

"You're planning on finding Selena tonight, too?"

"'Too'?" he echoed, as if he hadn't already guessed. He looked beyond her into the interior that appeared more inviting than she was. "Can I come in?"

But Reine stubbornly stood her ground. Apparently, she wasn't letting him off the hook without making him squirm.

"How did you know where to find me?" she asked, her gaze narrowing suspiciously. "How did you even know that I'd left the ranch?"

"I have my ways," he assured her, meaning a perfectly good set of eyes.

He'd been parked on the road edging Matlock Ranch, wondering whether or not he had it in him to brazen out another foray into forbidden territory to find her. He'd alternated between acting—which undoubtedly would have turned into a show—or simply calling her from the truck, using his cell phone. Of course, he'd known she could easily hang up on him. Therein had come his dilemma.

When he'd seen her car leave the property and turn onto the road, he'd been relieved of making a decision. Following her had been simple.

Then Cash had realized she'd been heading for Santa Fe. Figuring out her plans had been no challenge—they were obviously in sync. He figured she was planning to follow Tobiah's lead. No way would she have left her aunt's side otherwise.

"C'mon, Reine," he wheedled, pressing in on her close enough to distinguish her light scent from that of the garden. "Don't make me crawl."

He didn't miss her intake of breath or the flare in her eyes that she tried to hide by lowering her dark lashes.

She asked, "Does this mean we're working together for Gray's sake?"

And for my own, Cash thought, knowing he would have to appease her.

He nodded. "Okay, you got me. I've never been one to sit around and wait for something to happen."

"All right, then. Come in. I can be ready in a few minutes."

Cash raised his eyebrows. As far as he could tell, she was perfect now—hair coiled softly around a face so faultlessly made-up it looked natural. But he stepped inside without comment.

"You can wait in here," she said, already heading for a short hallway.

He stared after her for a moment, dealing with the reaction she kept provoking in him, as if he were the randy schoolboy she'd once known. He couldn't break the connection until she disappeared through another doorway—to her bedroom, no doubt. He forced himself to turn away before his imagination followed her inside.

The living room was cozy—with a brick fireplace flanked by mullioned windows, pine floor covered by a sisal rug, an old trunk/coffee table flanked by chairs upholstered in what looked to be Navajo rugs and a plain butter-yellow couch. A few pieces scattered here and there—baskets and pottery, a vase of fresh flowers and a bowl of cacti—reflected her simple, elegant taste.

The small, inviting room opened directly onto two nooks—a dining area in one direction, an office in the other.

He chose to explore the second.

Reine certainly had good taste, he thought, admiring the fine sugar-pine pieces.

Taking up one wall was a *trastero* with Mimbres patterns carved into the doors—frog, turtle, gecko and bear. He'd never seen anything quite like the cupboard. Neatly arranged bookshelves with a hand-tooled dimple adz crown stood opposite. And in between she'd placed a beautiful desk that caught his immediate interest.

Cash stooped to check out the mortise-and-tenon joinery, which would allow for expansion and contraction of the wood that had been carved with an El Rey pattern. He admired the careful workmanship. A friend of his Uncle Nemesio's did such work and he wondered if this piece had been crafted by the same man.

Rising, he was reminded of the odd exchange between his mother and Nemesio that morning. He couldn't forget his uncle implying that Gray's being dead might not be so bad....

He shook off the weird feeling the memory gave him and was about to leave the office area when a tooled leather-bound scrapbook on the desk caught his eye. He hesitated for only a second before switching on the tin lamp and flipping back the cover. Inside he found photographs and newspaper clippings. All were of kids, maybe ten to fifteen years old, who were at work in the community—hospitals and seniors' homes, day cares and after-school programs.

Reine herself was in some of the photos, and he caught her name in a few of the articles.

"Reine Kendrick, founder of Populace, a community-service project, gives troubled teens a new perspective on life with something positive to fill up their after-school hours...."

He checked out dates. The scrapbook had been started in 1990 and was currently up-to-date. He did some quick math and realized she must have established Populace directly out of college.

Juvenile delinquents. Kids in trouble. She gave them an alternative to a future in jail.

Why hadn't he known this about her? Why had he mistakenly assumed she would be content to live off her trust fund without purpose in her life?

Thoughtful, Cash closed the scrapbook and turned off the desk lamp.

He returned to the living room even as she called out, "Ready!"

He watched her swing back into the room, a Southwestern-print scarf draped over one shoulder, a small tooled-leather bag over the other. She seemed anxious, excited, a little unsure of herself.

"Did you drive by the plaza area before coming here?" she asked.

Every other woman he'd spent a moment with had suddenly paled beside her.

He nodded, for the moment rendered speechless and breathless by his realization.

"Well? Did you place it?"

He forced himself to concentrate on what she was saying. "What?"

"The gallery where we hope to find Selena."

"Enchanted," he murmured, and when her eyes widened, he clarified. "It's the name of a gallery. My guess is it's the one we're looking for."

What about what *he* was looking for?

THE GALLERY'S WINDOW display was exactly as Tobiah Hill had described it, Reine thought as they entered Enchanted. Those pueblo-shaped containers could be put to perfect use as new canisters for her kitchen.

Not that she should even consider making a purchase at the moment.

She glanced around at the half-dozen people in the gallery—all of whom seemed to be customers.

Disappointed, she complained, "I don't see anyone with dark, fiery hair."

"Just because the woman came in here doesn't actually mean she works here," Cash said. "She might have been a customer herself."

Reine's heart fell. "If that's true, we just ran into a brick wall."

"Unless Selena is a very important customer. Merchants tend not to forget them."

"Let's find out if we can," she said.

She spotted a young man who was straightening a display of handmade light-switch covers that were strewn across a table. He seemed to be the lone employee. About to say so, Reine realized Cash was no longer at her side.

She turned to see him checking over an unusual display of mirrors whose frames were decorated with snakes and lizards and birds of the Southwest.

And for a moment—while he was otherwise occupied—she checked him out from his handmade boots to his embroidered clay-colored shirt to his string tie whose silver clasp was set with garnet, topaz and citrine. His silver belt buckle and Concho hatband were nearly as fancy.

On the one hand, Cash appeared to be something of a dandy. On the other…

Remembering the encounter with her uncle, she shivered.

As if he realized she'd been staring at him, Cash turned to look at her. His gaze meshed with hers and played with her insides. She swallowed audibly.

"I'll catch up to you," he promised, glancing at the guy arranging the switch plates for a moment before turning toward another display.

"Fine. No problem," she muttered, wondering why he was acting so strangely.

From her immediate experience, she would have expected him to take charge of the situation. Undoubtedly, he would take over when he had a mind for it. In the meantime…

I can handle this, she thought.

She approached the gallery employee even as he put the last item in place.

"Can I help you?"

His smile seemed genuine, his expression open. He was young; just a kid, really. There was no need to be nervous.

Mentally holding her breath anyway, Reine said, "I'm looking for Selena."

His "She's not in right now," gave her heart. The woman *did* work here, after all.

Pulse thrumming, Reine asked, "Will she be in later?"

"I'm afraid not," he said.

"What about tomorrow morning?"

"I really can't guarantee it. Perhaps I can help you. Dominick Ptak."

"Thanks, but this is a personal matter."

"I'd be happy to take a message."

"Actually, I would prefer contacting Selena myself," Reine said smoothly. "Would you have her card with a number where I can reach her?"

Or where she could leave her own number in hopes the woman would contact her.

"Of course." Dominick moved to a work desk, pulled a business card from a holder and handed it to her. "Here you go, miss."

Reine took a quick glance: Enchanted—Selena Cullen, Owner. Relieved—this was even better than she'd hoped for—she smiled.

"Thanks."

She turned to find out why Cash hadn't been breathing down her neck. He was caught up inspecting an incredible adobelike sculpture/fireplace. The facade represented an animal—a bear, with claws protruding from the base and teeth from the top of the hearth.

Though it was quite striking, it wasn't her.

Not believing it was Cash, either, she came up behind him and whispered, "You're not thinking about buying, are you?" even as she handed him the business card.

"Why not?" Glancing at it, he raised his eyebrows. "It's one of a kind."

"Is that your primary criterion for wanting to own something?"

"Give me a better reason."

"How about because you love it and can't live without it," Reine suggested.

"How sentimental of you."

Choosing not to take that as a criticism, she glanced at the price and whistled softly. "Thirty-two thousand."

"It's only money."

Which Cash proceeded to spend.

The salesman was beside himself at what an incredulous Reine figured was probably one of the healthiest commissions he'd ever earned.

This was no doubt the reason why, before they had a chance to leave, he said, "By the way, if you two really need to talk to Selena tonight, you might check Green Chiles over on Cerrillos Road later. Her friend Dolores is the manager. Selena stops there most Friday nights before going home."

Cash saluted him. "Thanks for the tip, Dominick."

"No, thank *you,* Mr. Abreu!"

Reine waited until they'd hit the street before asking, "Does money get you everything you want?"

His gaze was intent on her when he said, "Not quite everything. But I give it my best shot."

"So I gather."

Thirty-two thousand for a tip on where to find Selena Cullen was a little hard to swallow....

Was it possible he would spend a small fortune on Gray's behalf? Maybe he had so much money it meant nothing to him. Or just maybe he saw the fireplace as an investment.

Reine couldn't help but be cynical where Cash Abreu was concerned. He'd given her enough reason to doubt him, starting all those years ago when he'd broken her trust.

True, he hadn't left Matlock Ranch of his own volition—even as it was true that he could have found a way to see her if that was what he'd really wanted. She'd awaited word from him. But all her waiting had been in vain. Even at Zane Abreu's funeral, Cash had chosen not to approach her.

He'd remained at his mother's side, staring at her through eyes empty of their having any future together.

All for one, and one for all...

How quickly he'd forgotten their covenant.

Reine stared at him, as if she could read beyond the facade he presented to the world. The store's lights splashed a warm glow through the dark. A golden haze settled on his face, softening his features, reminding her of the boy he used to be. But try as she did, she could discern no clear-cut answers to the many questions she still had.

Cash broke the quiet moment when he said, "I assume you want to head over to Green Chiles."

"You weren't thinking of leaving me behind."

"Not a chance."

Tonight he drove a Jaguar. Trying to ignore the warmth of Cash's hand as he helped her into the luxurious car, she slid into the passenger seat and inhaled the scent of leather. The anticipation she'd been experiencing since leaving Matlock Ranch still flowed rampantly through her. For the life of her, she couldn't say if it had to do with Selena Cullen or Cash Abreu.

Whether or not she wanted to admit as much, a familiar tension radiated between them. She wasn't foolish enough to deny it. But neither was she foolish enough to give in to something sure to lead nowhere. Luckily for her, Cash wasn't pushing. That would make the situation even more uncomfortable.

As he swung the car into Friday-night traffic, she asked, "What made you change your mind?"

"About Gray?"

"About admitting it." He'd been evasive all day. It was time he let down his guard, she thought. "Do you need so much control that you can't even share your feelings?"

"Maybe I don't have *any*."

Everyone has feelings, even him, she thought. "Or you learned to lie really well."

"I don't need to lie to anyone."

"Not even to yourself?" she asked.

"Why would I need to do that?"

"For the same reason a whole lot of people do—so you can live with yourself."

"That sounds like an insult."

"I'd rather think of it as being the simple truth," she countered.

"I haven't done anything wrong."

"You mean now."

"How far back should I go?"

Remembering the way he'd abandoned her and Gray without a thought to their feelings, she said, "Let your conscience be your guide."

"You seem to be doing a fine job of judging me. But what do you really know about my life, Reine? What makes you fit to criticize?"

"When did I say anything critical?"

"You didn't have to. Where you're concerned, my sixth sense is highly developed," Cash said. "I can practically read your thoughts."

"That's hard to believe. Maybe seventeen years ago—"

"Now."

"Prove it."

"You think I'm arrogant," he began, turning onto Cerrillos Road. "A little too obsessed with making money. Add spendthrift." He paused for a second, then asked, "How am I doing so far?"

"Clairvoyant," she admitted, laughing.

"Shall I go on?"

"Give it a rest. Besides, we're almost there."

They were passing motels and a variety of eateries—tourist row. The traffic seemed to be getting thicker. The following week it would be even worse when people arrived in droves to buy Native American artwork at the Indian Market.

A few minutes' drive brought them to Green Chiles, a restaurant and bar located in what had once been a private home. The rooms had been kept pretty much intact—size-wise, at least—so the multiple dining areas each had the feeling of intimacy. While she didn't get here often, this was one of Reine's favorite restaurants.

The moment Cash opened the heavy wooden door for her, the succulent odors of New Mexican home cooking wafted out over them. When her stomach growled in appreciation, Reine put a hand to her middle and willed it to stop.

"I heard that." Behind her as they entered, Cash stooped to speak softly in her ear. "You're starving, aren't you?"

"I'm fine."

It was a bold-faced lie. She *was* starving, and his pressing close to her was hard on her nerves.

"We'll get something to eat while we're here," he said as they joined the crowd in the foyer.

She glanced around at all the waiting customers.

The place was always crowded—and on the weekend it was nearly impossible to get a table without a reservation.

Having to raise her voice to be heard above the crowd noise in addition to the sound of live music coming from a nearby room, she said, "Don't count on getting a table."

"Don't count on my *not* getting one," he challenged.

Reine was looking for a comeback when she realized she was being silly. Sharing a meal with the man wouldn't kill her, and since she did have to eat eventually, she couldn't think of a better place.

"Fine."

When she saw the gleam of triumph in Cash's eyes, Reine regretted giving in so easily. She wondered if he always got his way.

Undoubtedly...

"Wait here," he said. "I'll be right back."

She watched him edge through the waiting customers to the hostess's desk, his hand slipping in and out of his pocket as he moved. A bribe, no doubt. He probably figured he could buy anything. And perhaps he could.

Then the crowd mostly swallowed her view of him as he talked to the woman in charge.

Reine wondered if this was Selena's friend, Dolores. If so, she didn't have much to say, because he was back in a flash.

"We'll be seated in a few minutes," Cash told her. "Selena's friend isn't even here at the moment. But once she arrives, the hostess will send her to our table."

"I'm impressed."

"Sounds more like 'disturbed' to me."

"Only a little. Naive person that I am, I normally wait my turn."

Cash shrugged. "Should I tell her to cancel that table?"

"No! I mean, we want to talk to Dolores about Selena, right?"

"Right."

For once, he let her off the hook.

MARLENE DIDN'T KNOW how long Jasper had been holed up in his office away from her, but she couldn't tolerate being alone anymore. Gray was their only son and she wanted—no, *needed*—her husband's support.

Her pulse throbbing, she braced herself for his animosity. All she wanted was a little reassurance from the man with whom she'd shared her bed for thirty-five years—surely not too much to ask.

She knocked at the study door before she lost her nerve.

"Go away!" came the shout from within.

Marlene opened the door anyway.

"What are you doing in the dark?" she asked softly.

She could see his silhouette. He was sitting at his desk.

Flicking on the wall switch, she flooded the room with light, making him squinch his eyes. Her gaze went past him to the desktop and to the bottle of whiskey that was nearly empty. He hadn't even bothered to replace the cap.

"Jasper, how long have you been drinking?"

"Not long enough!" he said defiantly.

Hearing the fear beneath the loud words, she moved to him and put a comforting hand on his shoulder.

"You're not the only one worried about Gray. You don't have to suffer alone."

"Not worried." He shrugged her hand away. "Gray's gonna be all right."

"You heard something?" she asked, but he couldn't look at her. The averted gaze confirmed it. "You did! When? Jasper!"

"This afternoon."

"And you didn't tell me?" she whispered brokenly, knowing he'd had his chance, but had forced another confrontation instead. She backed away from him. "How much?"

"Two million bucks by sundown Monday."

"Two million!" she echoed in horror.

"He knows I don't have the money. He knows Matlock Construction is gonna go under if I can't figure out how to stop it. Can't squeeze blood out of a stone."

Exactly what she'd been fearing.

"Why didn't *I* know?" Marlene asked him. "Why don't you talk to me about these things? Even so, surely there's something we can do—"

"Right. We're gonna wait."

"We *can't* wait!" Mind spinning, Marlene pressed her hands to her chest. She was having trouble breathing. "We have to get the money together somehow."

And she could think of only one way.

Papa would roll over in his grave—but he would have done it, she was certain. He'd loved Gray from the day his grandson was born, and a loved one was more important than any possession.

"The land," she said. "We'll have to sell it."

Jasper snorted. "The hell we will! That'd be playin' right into his hands. All part of the plan."

"What?" Marlene tried to focus on his ranting. "You're not making sense."

"He wants me to sell him the land and I won't, so he figures out a scheme where he forces me into it. He takes my son and demands money he knows I don't have. So I sell him the land to get the ransom. Here comes the irony—he gets his money back in trade for Gray. The whole thing costs him nothing. And me, everything."

"You're talking about Cash." *Again!* Why couldn't he be thinking about *their* son? "Why do you keep obsessing over this stupid feud?"

"Because he's guilty!" Jasper said, eyes blazing.

"That whelp vowed he'd do this to me. But I'll show him who has the smarts!"

"Cash wouldn't do this," she protested. Jasper had reason to feel guilty—maybe that was what was driving him to ignore the real situation. "Cash would never hurt Gray."

"Exactly!" He grimaced drunkenly. "That's where I got him. He wouldn't hurt the brother who's never done anything to him. Therefore, I don't gotta worry about Gray anymore, and I don't need to do a thing. Abreu will tire of the game and he'll let Gray go. All we have to do is wait."

Marlene grew colder with each word. And when he'd finished, she said, "No."

"What?"

"You're wrong, Jasper. You've never been so wrong in your life."

"The subject is closed, woman!"

"For you, maybe." She shook her head and backed away from the man whom she'd defended far too often. "Not for me."

Feeling as if her husband had ripped out her heart, Marlene ran from the study.

Part of the spread was hers.

As much as she loved this land that had been her home her entire life, she loved her only son far more. She would do anything for him, including selling everything she could get her hands on.

But...would it be enough?

Chapter Six

Reine couldn't help but enjoy being spoiled a bit after everything she'd been through the past two days.

A corner table in the coziest of rooms…Cash smoothly ordering a New Mexican platter for two as though he remembered all her favorite foods…the guitarist stopping at their table to play a disturbingly romantic piece…

They weren't on a date, she reminded herself.

Such high tension as she'd been enduring needed a release. That came along with their twenty-four-ounce drinks—gold margaritas with Grand Marnier floats.

"If I were a suspicious woman, I'd think you were trying to get me drunk."

"And I was certain that you *were* suspicious."

"Maybe," she admitted with a tired grin.

"To seeing Gray safely returned," Cash murmured, clinking his salt-limned glass to hers.

"To Gray's safety."

They both took long swallows. Reine closed her eyes for a moment and savored the pleasant sweet-sour taste. Tequila-induced warmth swam through her. It felt so good that she took another sip.

"You turned out as beautiful as I knew you would."

Startled not only by the compliment, but by the warm vibrancy of Cash's voice, Reine set down her glass and tried to keep her tone light. "Flatterer. But it's not like we haven't seen each other over the years."

"From afar," he agreed.

"That was *your* choice."

"What if I *choose* to close the distance between us?"

He was gazing at her so intently that her heart skipped a beat and she covered by picking up her drink and fortifying herself with another long swallow. What if he was serious? If he pursued her, could she resist?

"Why would you want to?" she then asked.

"Because you're one of a kind."

"Like that fireplace you bought?"

"Because I need someone like you in my life."

"'Someone' is pretty generic."

"Because I didn't even know how much I missed being with you, sharing something—"

"Awful?" she finished for him.

"— that makes me feel…different than I do normally, I guess."

It was amazing what a little tequila did to a man's tongue. Could be there was a beating heart in that broad chest, after all, Reine thought.

For a moment, Cash's expression was open—unguarded—and Reine felt as if she could see straight through to his soul. She sensed that, while he had everything tangible a man could desire, he was empty inside of the things that counted.

The good things.

The things she had recognized in him even at age ten, when she'd first been brought to the ranch by Aunt Marlene. That thirteen-year-old boy had been filled with joy and passion and loyalty. Now, all she sensed inside him was an open wound of a soul filled with bitterness and loneliness that he kept trying to patch with material goods.

It made her want to weep.

"So, what do you think, Reine?" he asked when she'd been quiet for too long. "About you and me."

"I think you can't depend on another person for your own happiness."

"I can try."

"Happiness comes from within, Cash. It comes from knowing you're the best you can be. Inside, where it counts. It means living for the now."

"I do that."

"And for the future."

"I'm building my future every day."

"Most of all, it means letting go of the past."

He was silent for a moment before quietly asking, "You're saying I should let go of you?"

Reine shook her head. "You don't have me to let go of in the first place, Cash. You made certain of that, years ago. Your money may be able to buy you a lot of things, but I don't happen to be one of them."

"You're that rich?"

Coming from someone else, the question might have shocked her. But she was getting used to the way Cash thought strictly in terms of dollars.

"In the things that count, yes, I am rich. As for money—that doesn't really matter."

"You can say that because you've always had it."

Now she was shocked. "What in the world gave you *that* idea?"

"You used to brag about the trust fund that you inherited from your mother."

Reine might have laughed if the truth weren't so sad. "Right. The trust fund." The one her father had drained until her mother had refused to let him touch another penny, after which he'd done his own disappearing act.

She'd inherited what had been left, all right— enough to see her through college, provide a down payment on a modest house and endow Populace with seed money. The limited principal had run out years ago, but Cash didn't need to know that.

"My trust fund did give me a decent start in life," she said. "For which I am very grateful."

The food came then, and Reine dug in, her appetite fueled by the drink. She devoured a pork tamale and half a chicken enchilada before realizing Cash was merely picking at his *carne asada.* He seemed to be concentrating on his margarita instead of his steak. And on his thoughts.

Reine left him to them, figuring he needed a little space to consider what had been, in the end, a rejection. For, unless he was willing to change, she wasn't ready to let him into her life, no matter how strong the attraction between them. She guessed he needed a few minutes to comprehend that.

And so she wasn't ready for him saying, "So tell me what you know about the problems at Matlock

Construction,'' making her feel as if she'd just been thrown a curveball.

Here she was, starting to relax—starting to feel mentally in tune with him—and Cash had to go and ruin it by pumping her for information about her uncle's business. Her appetite suddenly gone, she sat back in her chair and stared.

How could he be so callous?

''Do you really think I would betray the confidence of the people I love for a drink, a dinner and a proposition of sorts?'' she asked.

'' 'Betray'? I thought you wanted to figure out what happened to Gray.''

''What does the construction company have to do with the kidnapping?''

''Maybe nothing. I'm just playing the angles.''

''Isn't that what you've been doing all along?'' she demanded. ''Uncle Jasper claims you've single-handedly tried to ruin his business.''

''Not single-handedly. There are other aggressive competitors in our field. Wayne Albright, Evan Bixler and John Lonato, to name a few. I wonder if any of these men has reason to go after Matlock on a personal level.''

Bixler—why was that name so familiar? Reine wondered.

Cash was saying, ''Try to remember anything Matlock might have said about them,'' when a dark-haired woman approached their table.

''I was told you wanted to see me. Dolores Zaldava,'' the woman introduced herself. ''No complaints about the food or service, I hope.''

''None at all,'' Cash said, immediately standing.

He pulled out a vacant chair. "Would you join us for a moment?"

"Certainly." She took the offered seat. "So, what can I do for you?"

"We're looking for Selena Cullen," Reine said. "We stopped by Enchanted. Dominick told us we might be able to find Selena here."

"Oh. I'm not expecting her tonight. Actually, I haven't heard from her in days."

And Reine could tell that disturbed the manager. Odd. Neither her employee nor her good friend seemed to know what Selena Cullen was up to.

"Could Selena be out of town?" Cash asked.

"No. I mean…I don't think so. She didn't say, exactly." Dolores looked from one to the other. "Your seeing her—it's important?"

"Very," Reine assured the manager. "I hope nothing is wrong."

"Oh, dear, surely not. She's had enough grief lately with Jimmy's death, and all. I can't imagine what it would be like to lose one of my kids."

"Her son died?" Cash interjected. "How recently?"

Dolores sat back and stared at him. "There I go, talking out of school, again. I assumed you were Selena's friends. How did you say you know her?"

"We didn't," Reine admitted. "It's a friend-of-a-friend kind of thing."

"And just which friend might that be? Who *are* you?"

Watching carefully for her reaction, Reine said, "My name is Reine Kendrick. Jasper Matlock is my uncle."

The manager's expression immediately closed.

"You'll forgive me, but I must take care of a few things." She pushed herself away from the table and rose. "If I hear from Selena, I'll tell her you're looking for her."

On that note, she spun on her heel and walked straight out of the room.

"Odd reaction, don't you think?" Cash commented.

"She doesn't like Uncle Jasper, that's for certain."

"Too bad we didn't get a few more minutes with her. She obviously has some clue as to what was going on between him and Selena Cullen."

"Poor woman," Reine murmured, thinking about her loss. She could imagine how hard Aunt Marlene would take it if she were to lose Gray. "Maybe it's just as well we didn't find her."

"At least not until we learn exactly how her son died."

CASH CALLED UP THE obituary from the Santa Fe *Sun* via the Internet. Wanting to satisfy his curiosity about Jimmy Cullen's death, he'd brought Reine to the Cash Development offices to let his state-of-the-art equipment get the information for them. He sat behind his desk while she set herself as far from the computer—and him—as possible.

"I found it," he told her.

"What does it say?" She roused herself from the leather chair in the seating area and drew closer.

Cash quickly scanned the short paragraph. "Nothing significant but the date of death and that he made his home in Española. Let's see what else I can find."

He set up a new search and was quickly rewarded

with links to several articles about Cullen's death. He called up the one with the latest information.

"Here we go." He skimmed and related the story in shorthand fashion. "James Cullen found dead in his apartment by the cleaning woman.... Christ... only twenty-eight years old and he committed suicide!"

Why? He'd have had his whole life ahead of him.

"Did he leave a note?" Reine asked, now standing directly behind him.

As she looked over his shoulder, her hip pressed against his back. The room suddenly shrank. Cash had to force himself to concentrate.

"No note. But suicide was the medical examiner's finding. And the authorities suggested that Cullen had gone into a severe depression due to a failed business."

Her voice was a little shaky when Reine asked, "What kind of business?"

"A fledgling heating and air-conditioning outfit." He continued to scan the article and knew she wasn't going to like the rest. "Seems Matlock Construction bought him out for peanuts."

Reine caught her breath. "Uncle Jasper was involved?"

"Don't sound so horrified. Like I told you before, it's just business." Cash couldn't believe he was actually defending the very man he'd been in the process of ruining. "Bigger companies eat up little ones or run them into the ground every day. It's not like he killed Jimmy Cullen. Or that he had any clue the guy would go off his rocker over a failed business."

"But Selena Cullen must blame Uncle Jasper for

his death, right? Undoubtedly that's why they had that confrontation in public.''

''Could be,'' he said.

''This sounds awful, I know…but in a way, I'm relieved. Not about anyone dying, of course. I mean, I thought Uncle Jasper and Selena were having an…''

When she couldn't seem to finish, Cash said, ''So did I.'' He couldn't miss the tears filling her eyes.

''It's just that I'm relieved for Aunt Marlene is all.''

Cash nodded. Of course he understood.

Gathering more details from the article, he was bothered by the particular June date of this company takeover. It came on the heels of Cash Development's taking over a small subsidiary of Matlock Construction a few weeks before—another heating and air-conditioning company—part of Cash's plan to cripple Matlock financially.

Cash sat back and thought about it.

He'd finagled a company out of Matlock, so the old man had turned around and done the same to someone weaker. And then the young man had turned around and eaten a gun.

The degree of separation between him and the late Jimmy Cullen was too close for Cash's comfort—not that *he* was responsible for the death, either, he told himself.

But where did culpability begin and where did it end? he wondered.

He also wondered what kind of a woman this Selena Cullen might be. Could she be tough enough to exact revenge? A son for a son?

A cold sweat enveloped him as he viewed the remaining articles without really digesting any new information.

Suddenly remembering Reine, he saw that she'd gone back to her chair. She seemed withdrawn. Depressed. Drowning in her own thoughts.

The same ones he kept having about Gray?

Closing down his computer, he said, "Hey, I think I'm ready for another margarita. A serious one, this time."

Reine started as if she had forgotten him, as well. Coming out of her trance, she rose and, brow furrowed, concentrated on straightening some invisible wrinkle or other in her skirt.

"A drink sounds tempting," she admitted, keeping her gaze directed everywhere but at him. "But if we're serious about finding Gray, we probably should call it a night."

She was probably right.

Not that he was counting on getting any sleep.

The degree-of-separation theory that gave Selena Cullen power over Gray because of something *he'd* started was tearing Cash up inside.

What if Matlock had been right and he *was* the one to blame for Gray's plight?

ALL FOR ONE AND ONE for all…

They were crawling through the dark, dank tunnel, one after the other—Cash taking the lead as always, Gray bringing up the rear behind Reine—all determined to find the opening on the other side.

There had always been stories about the cave mouth cut into a slope and cleverly concealed by a large rock outcropping in the hills near the chile mill; about the subterranean passages that went all the way to Black Mesa, ten miles distant, with other openings along the way. But no one had ever discovered the cave that they knew of.

Not until now.

Cash had been the one to find the opening, to convince them to explore inside, to choose which twists and turns to take. He never faltered. Never doubted himself. Never doubted them.

"I don't think this is such fun," Reine said as the tunnel began narrowing around them. "It's kinda spooky."

Not that she stopped or asked them to quit.

"There's nothing to be scared about!" Cash insisted, though he paused and turned as best he could, aiming their only flashlight back at them.

Gray was practically blinded by the light and had to squint to see anything of the two ahead of him.

Eleven-year-old Reine was never afraid of anything—or at least, nothing she would admit to. So if she said it, she was past scared, as the glimpse of her face convinced him.

"I don't like this place, either," Gray immediately piped up. "Let's go back."

"You got to be kidding!" Cash groused.

"Uh-uh. I just didn't want to say anything first," Gray lied for Reine's sake.

If Cash guessed otherwise, he didn't say. He didn't argue about it, either.

"All right. But I don't see any place up ahead where we can turn around. You'll have to back out."

"Okay by me."

"Me, too," Reine said, relief in her voice.

Gray started to crawl backward, and could hear more than see the others follow.

Cash was always fair. Always took others' needs into consideration. Always put him and Reine first.

He didn't admire anyone more.

He only wished they could be brothers instead of secret friends.

GRAY WOKE IN A SWEAT. In the dark. Feeling as if the walls of the abandoned gristmill were closing in on him the way that tunnel had done to Reine.

He'd never gone back there. Not alone. And not because he'd been afraid to, but because of the pact.

He wasn't a kid anymore. He now knew that he and Cash were brothers. Cash knew it, too; but once armed with the knowledge, he'd run from the fact.

All for one and one for all.

Gray was the one in trouble this time. Only this time he'd have to figure his own way out.

Though Cash and Reine had been here earlier, the old magic between the three of them was apparently gone, or they would have sensed how close he was and found him.

Besides, he couldn't count on Cash anymore.

And Reine was too foolish where her own welfare was concerned. She would rush into things, heart rather than head first. She would push past her fear and get herself hurt.

He struggled onto an elbow and scooted his body around until he could feel the lump beneath the edge of the bedroll. When his kidnappers had returned earlier, they'd let him relieve himself outside. He'd managed to pick up a nice sharp stone.

But then they'd sedated him again. He'd been asleep for some while now. He didn't know how long.

He positioned the stone so he could saw the ropes against it when he heard the hoofbeats.

Damn!

Frustration welled in him as he hid the stone under the bedroll again and scooted back around into a supine position.

One of them was back and his escape plan would have to be put on hold for a while longer.

CASH INSISTED ON SEEING her inside and Reine didn't argue. She was spooked by the knowledge of Jimmy Cullen's suicide and didn't really want to be alone.

"If you still want that drink…"

"If I didn't have to drive…"

Was Cash looking for a polite way to get away? Or was he looking for something else altogether?

Testing, Reine suggested, "How about a cup of tea for the road?"

"Sounds good."

He probably hated tea, she thought, leading the way into the kitchen. Maybe he just didn't want to be alone any more than she did.

"Great room," he said.

His appreciative tone made her smile.

"I had it renovated when I bought the place. I've always thought of the kitchen as being the heart of a home. A person should want to spend time in it."

"Then it's a success."

As Reine filled the kettle with water, she noticed him inspecting one of the freestanding cabinets designed so it could be moved around according to her whim. Mostly of stained wood, it was accented with painted insets and a whimsical "snake" handle.

Other Southwestern animals had been added to each of the cabinets.

"I had them custom-made," she said.

"So I see." He hunkered down to take a closer look. "By the same craftsman who built your desk?"

"As a matter of fact, yes." Impressed that he'd made the connection, too aware of his every move, of the way his trousers stretched across his thighs, of the way his shirt strained across his back, she said, "I noticed you have good taste in handcrafted furniture yourself."

While Cash ran delicate fingers over the design carved into the wood, Reine wrapped her arms around her middle.

His voice low and husky, he said, "I learned to appreciate real quality when I was living and working with Nemesio."

"Like adobe buildings."

He rose and nodded. "Like that." His expression bemused, he said, "Uh, the kettle…"

Flustered, Reine suddenly realized the kettle was overflowing. She shut off the water and set the kettle on the stove. Then, going for a safe topic, she asked, "So, do you think Selena Cullen could be the one?"

"Could be, although I have trouble picturing a middle-aged city woman riding in on a man's own territory, taking him hostage and covering her tracks as she goes." He moved closer and set a hip against the counter's edge. "If she's the one behind Gray's disappearance, she had to have had some reliable help."

"How does one get that kind of help?"

"Money can buy anything."

Hating the cynicism in his tone, she argued, "Not

anything. At least, not the things that count. But illicit hirelings, yes, I'm sure. The question is, how do you find someone willing to become a kidnapper? Advertise?''

''My guess would be by asking around. Recommendations from friends and associates. We don't have a clue as to Selena's background. Who she knows.''

''She knows Uncle Jasper.'' And part of Reine was still wondering how well. ''Maybe I should ask him.''

''Brave girl. Why do you imagine he'd tell you anything? You have more confidence in his willingness to cooperate than I do.''

''It would be in his own self-interest. He's desperate over Gray.''

Cash nodded but didn't reply, and Reine realized that he was suddenly down-in-the-mouth quiet.

''What?'' she asked softly. ''I didn't say anything you didn't already know.''

'''Self-interest,''' he echoed. ''Mine. I'm beginning to think there could be long-term consequences to every action one takes—things you never counted on happening.''

''Such as?''

''Such as my taking over one of Matlock's subsidiaries eventually resulting in Gray's disappearance.''

She leaned a hip on the counter next to him. ''I don't get it.''

''It was a heating and air-conditioning company. I took over Matlock's, so he took over Cullen's....''

Grasping his train of thought, Reine tried to reassure Cash. ''Like you said, it's business.''

But that didn't keep the possible connection from bothering her, as well. She felt no conviction in her words of comfort. If it was true…

How horrible, and not only for Gray.

Cash looked so despondent, she put her arms around him just as easily as she would have done years ago, without first considering the consequences.…

Slowly, he responded, his arms encircling her back, allowing her to move away if she would.

Heat simmered along her flesh—a welcome, life-affirming heat. The sensation was at once calming and disturbing. Familiar and alien. Seductive and dangerous.

''Reine,'' he whispered, his lips in her hair.

Confused, she didn't know whether to push him away or to pull him closer. Instead of doing either, she closed her eyes and freed her mind from its jumble of confusion.

The years tumbled away.… Fifteen again, she was wildly in love for the first and only time of her life.

And so, when he moved his head, his lips trailing her jaw to her mouth, she couldn't protest.

She didn't want to.

She *wanted* his mouth covering hers, claiming her, opening her, outside and in.

The touch of his tongue on hers sizzled with promise that started at her head and worked its way down to her toes, licking every nerve in between. His hands moved to the small of her back, then slipped lower, pulling her to him. He pressed hard against her belly until he cupped her bottom, reshaped and fitted her to him.

After which he turned to trap her against the cabinet, angling her so he could pin her there while freeing his hands. The silk blouse and satin bra were no barrier to his touch. Through the thin layers of material, he palmed her, squeezed her, tormented her.

Her limbs turned liquid and she clung to him to remain upright. Fully clothed, in the middle of her kitchen, she was being made love to and loving every second of it.

His hands stroked down her chest and belly to her waist, then moved around her hips. He began tugging on the material of her skirt, hiking it up, bunching it around her waist. The air laved her naked legs like a lover's caress. A soft moan escaped her lips and her fingers dug into his back.

He reached under her to assault her panties from behind—hooking one finger beneath the elastic, then another—sliding them around and under her buttocks.

He rocked his hips and slid his hand farther under her, thereby assaulting her from both directions at once. Unable to help herself, she hung on to him with both arms, curled her legs around his thighs and arched against him.

His mouth against her neck, he murmured, ''I want you.''

She wanted him, too. *Most* of her did. But a tiny part—the part with the memory of how he'd abandoned her and of what he'd become—shrilled a warning.

Caution!

Stop. Now.

While she still could.

But the shrill noise continued, penetrating the fog of desire that was clouding her mind.

The kettle—it was steaming!

As was she.

Freeing her mouth and pressing her hands against his chest to put a few inches between them was one of the hardest things she'd ever made herself do.

"The tea."

"I'd rather have you."

"Even you can't always have what you want," she said, untangling herself from his embrace.

"But you're the one who asked me what I wanted to help you...."

Unable to tell whether or not he was joking, Reine backed away and busied herself with the kettle, her hands shaking slightly as she poured water into the teapot and set out the mugs. Her heart was pounding and not only because of the hot embrace they'd shared.

Surely Cash hadn't actually agreed to help her in exchange for sexual favors. He'd given her enough hints over the past two days. Remembering she'd been almost desperate enough to offer herself didn't make her feel any better.

She wanted it to be about Gray, not about her.

About loyalty, not about seduction.

About love, not about possession.

What did Cash *really* want?

Though she yearned to ask him, fear kept her silent. She didn't want to hear the wrong words—the ones that would shatter the little bit of renewed faith she had in him.

"How do you like yours?" she asked as the tea leaves steeped in the pot.

"Any way I can get it."

Their eyes met and she knew he wasn't talking about the tea. Feeling her temperature rise, she deliberately slammed a sugar bowl in front of him and moved to the refrigerator. He'd always liked to fluster her. To make her blush.

"I have both lemon and cream," she said as calmly as she could manage.

When Reine glanced back, Cash wasn't looking at her but at a spot to her right. "Shouldn't you check your messages?" he asked.

She followed his gaze. "Oh, no. I didn't even notice."

With trepidation, she approached the answering machine whose red light blinked at her accusingly. Only one person had called. Certain that this was about Gray, she hit the message button and held her breath as the tape rewound and sprang to life.

"We heard from the k-kidnapper," came her aunt's shaky voice. "Reine...i-it isn't good. He wants two m-million dollars...and Jasper says we don't have it to g-give."

"Oh, Lord," Reine murmured as her aunt sobbed out loud.

"Jasper isn't going to do anything to get the m-money, either. He won't let go of his obsession. He insists Gray will be all right b-because Cash has him...."

Cash's low curse startled her, but she didn't blame him for being angry—not one bit.

"I have to get my hands on the money s-somehow, Reine. I'm going to do whatever I must, even if it means going against m-my husband. I have to save my child...."

More crying—softer, but desperate.

Then, because Marlene didn't speak again, the machine cut her off.

Leaving Reine stunned.

"Dear God, two million dollars!" she whispered.

A lot of money, but Uncle Jasper had a lot of resources. Or used to. Something had to be terribly wrong. He would never refuse to do what he had to for Gray. Could it be there was no way he could get his hands on the money and so had fabricated the excuse about Cash in his desperation?

But...

"Aunt Marlene seemed to think she could get her hands on that kind of money," Reine mused aloud. "How?"

"Calling in favors?"

Reine whirled on Cash. "Listen to yourself! Everything isn't a business, you know. This is life we're talking about, here!"

Life and death...

"But in this instance, Gray's life does come down to money," Cash reminded her. "And a lot of it."

Reine knew only one person who would have no trouble producing two million dollars. She stared at Cash. He stood back, his expression oddly impassive. She couldn't even hazard a guess as to his thoughts.

But her own mind was following a single track: What would it take to convince an embittered, greedy man to buy back his brother's freedom and possibly his life?

Chapter Seven

Cash mulled over the content of the message from Marlene Matlock. "She didn't say how long."

"What?" Reine whispered, her expression confused. She appeared to be coming out of a shocked stupor.

"How much time she has to come up with the money."

"No, she didn't. I'd better return her call and find out."

Reine grabbed the phone and punched in the number.

Watching her, Cash wiped a shaky hand over his face. Two million. That was damn serious money. Even he would be hard-pressed to come up with that kind of cash.

What the hell was Matlock going to do?

Nothing! According to his wife, at least.

He'd rather sit around and blame the son he'd always wished had never been born.

"Aunt Marlene," Reine was saying tightly, "I, uh, got your message. Please call me as soon as you can."

And what could Matlock do even if he weren't being such a fool? Cash wondered.

Thanks to his own concerted endeavors—and to the contributing efforts of smart businessmen always willing to take advantage of weakened competition—the old man's company was teetering. Cash figured he probably had resorted to pouring his personal resources into Matlock Construction. Undoubtedly, he was strapped.

Crossing the kitchen toward him, her arms wrapped around her middle, Reine said, "Maybe I should go back to the ranch right away."

Cash thought of telling her to stay put but figured that would only spur her to go against his wishes. Instead, he chose calm logic.

"What if your aunt is sleeping?" he suggested. "You'll awaken her for nothing. Besides, you could use some rest. You look too exhausted to drive."

Cash wanted to lift her into his arms and carry her to bed himself, but he knew any good intentions would dissipate the moment he touched her.

"Besides," he added, "what kind of help will you be to her if you're too tired to think clearly?"

"You're right," she said. "And what can anyone do in the middle of the night? I suppose first thing in the morning will be soon enough."

"To call, anyway."

"What do you mean, 'call'?"

"As in connecting via telephone. Holding her hand isn't going to get things done. I thought we were committed to figuring out who's behind this scheme. Considering the stakes, don't you agree it's more important than ever?''

That was part of it, Cash knew. He could manage what needed doing alone. Being honest with himself, however, Cash admitted to an ulterior motive. He wanted Reine, and his getting her wasn't going to happen long-distance. He wasn't welcome on Matlock land, so the less time she spent there, the better for his cause.

''What if we still can't find Selena Cullen?'' she asked him. ''Then what?''

''First of all, Selena being a suspect doesn't make her guilty.''

''I know that.''

''So we have to keep looking at other possibilities,'' Cash insisted, ''and I'd say our timetable was just moved up. Who's the equivalent of Tobiah Hill at Matlock Construction?''

''You mean like a foreman?''

''I mean someone who knows everything that goes on in that company.''

''That would be Nora, I guess,'' Reine told him. ''Nora Archer is Uncle Jasper's executive assistant.''

''Sounds like she's our woman—that is, if we can we get her to talk. Would she see doing so as being disloyal to Matlock?''

''She might.... On the other hand, she's always been fond of Gray.''

''How well do *you* know her?''

''Well enough.''

''Then it'll be up to you to convince her Gray's life is more important than some confidentiality issue.''

Reine nodded. "I'll contact Nora first thing in the morning."

"Our paying her a surprise visit might be more effective," Cash suggested.

"Together?"

"That would be the plan," he agreed. "If we show up on her doorstep, it'll be a lot harder for her to say no. She won't have time to think. Won't have time to call her boss and alert him."

He could only imagine Matlock's explosive reaction. A perverse part of him would like to be a fly on the wall to see that one.

"I suppose you have a point," Reine conceded.

"So where do we find her on a Saturday?"

"Nora and her husband have a small piece of property just outside Española."

Which was quite a bit closer to Chimayo than Santa Fe. He considered their options.

"Where shall I meet you?" she asked. "At your place?"

"What's wrong with right here?"

"I have to get over to the ranch sometime tomorrow, anyway," she argued. "And why would you want to drive all the way back to Santa Fe?"

"Who said anything about driving back?" Cash moved a little closer and ran a finger up the side of her arm. "I don't have to leave at all."

Reine licked her lips. "Yes, you do," she said a bit breathlessly.

So she wasn't going to sleep with him. Yet. They were equally in lust, but he was the only one being honest about it. As far as he was concerned, it was a done deal. Her nerves told him so. He could be patient for as long as it took. Still, he couldn't give in so easily.

"I'm a man who knows how to compromise. That couch of yours looks perfectly comfortable."

"It is, but you're not invited to try it."

"You'd rather have me in your bed, then?"

"I didn't say that!"

She was squirming and, callous creature that he knew himself to be, he was enjoying every second of her discomfort. He ran the side of his thumb along the line of her jaw and was rewarded by her quick intake of breath.

"I don't know, Reine. I felt pretty welcome a little while ago."

"That was a mistake."

"No mistake."

If she didn't want the same thing he did, she would come right out and say so, he was certain. He slipped his hand around the back of her neck, where the silk of her fallen hair teased his knuckles.

"I'm giving you fair warning," he went on softly. "I want you and I mean to have you."

She slapped his hand away and pushed past him and through the door into the hallway, muttering, "What either of us wants isn't important right now."

At least she wasn't denying the obvious.

"That's why you're throwing me out?"

"If I don't, neither of us will get any sleep."

Knowing he'd probably pushed as far as he should, Cash finally conceded. "All right. I'll leave and I'll even put that other discussion on hold—for now. But I'll be back in the morning, first thing."

"I'll meet you at the truck stop outside Española," she countered.

Cash stared at her intently, but she didn't back down. Her body language and stubborn expression told him she was set on having her own way. He guessed he would give it to her.

This time.

MARLENE HAD BEEN UP FOR hours, waiting for sunrise. At the first flow of dawn across the horizon, she left the house.

Her departure went unchallenged.

Jasper had undoubtedly passed out in his study. Either that or he'd used a guest room. This had been one of the few times in their marriage when she'd locked him out of their bedroom.

Not that where he chose to sleep would be an issue for much longer.

Starting up the car, she got onto the road as the sky lightened to a luminous blue, streaked with morning mauve. She wasn't going far. Sam Valdez's place was only a few miles down the road.

Jasper would have a stroke if he knew.

As far as she was concerned, he could just have one. It would serve him right.

He'd never loved her; had only married her to get his name on the land with water rights, and in the process, had handed off the woman carrying his child to his foreman. She hadn't known about Luna then, or she would never have conceded to her father's wishes.

She and Sam had always been neighbors. And once—twice, really—they'd been more.

As she turned onto his land, a flurry of butterflies made her queasy. She clutched the steering wheel and took a deep breath. Why should she expect more of him than she could get from her own husband. From Gray's own father.

It'll be all right, she promised herself, despite her uncertainty.

She drove up to the century-old hacienda looking for signs of life. Unless he'd changed, Sam was an early riser. A glimmer of light shone from the kitchen, and as she cut her engine, she was certain he'd come to the window.

By the time she arrived at the front door, he'd beaten her to it. The antique wooden panel swung wide.

"Marlene."

"Sam."

The years fell away as they stood there, staring at each other. For one moment, she was projected back to her youth, when she and Sam had kept company in secret.

His last name being Valdez, he hadn't been a suitable match according to her autocratic father. Although the Spaniards had settled the territory and had obtained the original land grants, eventually a Hispanic heritage had become something less than respectable to many of the late-coming, power-wielding Anglos. Her father had been one of them.

Besides which, Sam's father and hers had been sworn enemies—and all over the land that seemed to hold some kind of curse.

But Sam had been the one to help her through the loss of her mother when she'd been barely eighteen. Papa eventually had learned of that youthful relationship and had ended it.

"Come in," Sam said, stepping back to let her enter. "I was just getting breakfast together."

"Smells good."

"When was the last time you ate?"

"Yesterday, I guess." She wrinkled her forehead, trying to remember. She hadn't been hungry since Gray disappeared. "I'm sure I ate sometime."

"Well, I have enough on the stove to share, if you're in the mind for it."

She was.

A few minutes later, Marlene was seated in the kitchen, sipping at a mug of coffee, watching Sam tend to his potatoes in one pan, ingredients for an omelet in the other.

Sam Valdez wasn't as handsome as Jasper. He never had been. But there was a rugged quality about him that appealed to a woman. Lots of women. He'd had enough of them—rumors abounded when people got bored.

But Sam had never remarried after his divorce and Marlene had always wondered why.

As if it were yesterday, she remembered the second time they'd taken up with each other.

Seventeen years ago, Zane Abreu had died, leaving Cash the truth of his parentage in writing, and as a result, her safe world with Jasper had changed forever. His own wife having recently left him, Sam had gotten her through that period of devastation, as well.

"So, what brings you here, Marlene?" Sam asked, as he set two dishes on the plank table.

"Gray."

"Figured as much." He took a forkful of egg and followed it with a chunk of potato. "You decided to take me up on my offer?"

Her mouth full, Marlene swallowed and nodded.

"What can I do for you?"

"It's what we can do for each other," she stated far more calmly than she was feeling. "You get me the money I need to buy my boy's safety...." *If only Jasper hadn't left this to her.* "And I'll get you the land along the river you've always wanted."

Sam's fork clattered to his plate. "Jasper agreed to sell?"

"He doesn't have to. The land's mine."

"Not the way he tells it."

"Jasper is co-owner," she agreed, "as long as I stay married to him. Papa had his lawyer set it all up like a business arrangement."

Though she was fuzzy on the details. She'd never paid attention to the actual contract, for she'd never imagined she would have reason to turn her back on her husband. But Papa had assured her that if things didn't work out between her and Jasper, he wouldn't be able to walk away with what belonged to her and her children.

Jasper had been desperate enough for the land and all the opportunities that would come with it to agree to anything Papa demanded.

"Are you saying what I think you are?" Sam's expression was intent. "Are you telling me you're finally divorcing Jasper Matlock?"

"I'll do whatever I have to." If Jasper wouldn't agree to sell, she would take the decision from him. "I want my son alive and whole."

"How much do you need and when?" His words were exactly what she'd hoped to hear.

Marlene took a deep breath. "Two million dollars by Monday sunset."

"Two million!" Sam's eyes went huge. "I mean, the property's worth it, but I don't have that kind of money myself. And mortgages take time even if I could get me one that big. I'll just have to find another way.''

''Then you've agreed to help me?''

''I'll do my best for you, Marlene, just like I always have. I'll find a way as long as you don't look too closely at what I got to do to get what you need.''

Ignoring a warning twinge, she selfishly said, ''I want my son safe.''

''Have you spoken to Gray? Made sure for yourself he's all right?''

Tears sprang to her eyes even though she'd told herself she wouldn't cry anymore.

''I must have been sleeping when the call came in. By the time I found out, Jasper was too drunk to make much sense.''

''Damn fool!'' Sam groused. ''And what about that niece of yours?''

''Reine? What about her?''

''Did she carry through with whatever plan was going through her pretty head?''

''I don't know,'' Marlene said, unable to miss his intent expression. ''I haven't spoken to her since early last evening. I assume if she discovered anything of importance, she would have contacted me....''

Sam shrugged. ''She probably went home and forgot about it, then.''

''Oh, I doubt it. Reine doesn't give up so easily. She'll keep at something until she succeeds. Though this time, I believe she's in over her head.''

''Maybe you ought to talk some sense into the girl before she gets herself hurt.''

Marlene shuddered at the thought. She couldn't

bear to see something happen to her niece. Reine was almost as dear to her as her own son.

"I should talk to her," she agreed.

Though Marlene suspected that, despite whatever she said, Reine would continue on her chosen path and just not say anything that would worry her.

Which, perhaps, she already was doing....

REINE DROVE INTO THE truck-stop parking lot looking for Cash's vehicle of the day. She hadn't asked him what he'd be driving, but she was certain the Jaguar wouldn't be de rigueur.

In addition to several eighteen-wheelers, all she spotted were some pickups and a pair of vintage low riders for which Española was famous. These were particularly fancy, one having an Aztec pyramid painted across the trunk, and the other, skeletons playing musical instruments.

There was no sign of Cash.

Deciding she might as well wait inside, she first found the rest room to freshen up. Then, about to enter the restaurant, she spotted Ozzie Skinner at a booth arguing with a fair-haired man whose back was to her.

What was the ranch hand doing here when he should be on the job? Remembering his having complained about his back to Tobiah Hill, she wondered if he hadn't defied the foreman, after all, and had decided to take whatever time he chose—not that his back seemed to be bothering him at the moment.

Intent on the men in the booth, she didn't hear the one come up behind her until he said, "There you are. I was wondering where you'd taken yourself."

She turned to Cash. "And I was wondering where *you* were, *period.*"

His eyebrows arched. "You missed me. Good."

"Don't flatter yourself."

Seeming amused, he indicated the restaurant. "Hungry?"

"I had breakfast. I just thought I'd grab a cup of coffee while I was waiting for you," she said, glancing back at Skinner and his companion.

"Something wrong?"

"I'm just wondering what Ozzie Skinner's up to."

Cash followed her gaze. "He doesn't look too happy, does he? Maybe Tobiah fired him."

"Could be."

"Still want that coffee?"

"To go?"

"Fine with me."

"I'll take mine with cream."

Cash stepped up to the counter to place their order while Reine hung back, her attention once more straying toward the booth. Both men had risen and the fair-haired one was already stalking toward the cash register. His handsome face was marred by a small but nasty scar that drew up one side of his mouth in a perpetual snarl. Though he seemed vaguely familiar, she couldn't place him.

Even as she stared, he flicked his pale gaze over her in disinterest.

Not so Skinner.

The moment the ranch hand spotted her, he started and quickly turned away, stuffing his hat on his bald head and his unlit cigar into his mouth.

Maybe Tobiah hadn't fired him, after all. Undoubtedly he was afraid she'd tell the foreman she'd seen him here when he should have been working.

As if she didn't have more important things on her mind.

Both men were gone by the time Cash handed her a paper cup filled with coffee.

He insisted on taking only one vehicle—his, of course—and Reine saw no reason to object. She slid into the leather passenger seat of his pickup and, sipping her coffee, contented herself with giving him directions. They arrived at their destination before she'd even finished her cup.

She gazed around at the Archer property. The few acres were fenced. Two horses grazed in a pasture near a lean-to shelter. The house itself was a modest two-story affair with a territorial-style overhang porch the length of the building.

Cash pulled up the gravel drive and stopped behind a car with a vanity license plate that read NORA 4, saying, "Looks like she's home."

"But is she awake?"

"If not, we'll be an even bigger surprise than we anticipated."

But to Reine's relief, Nora Archer was awake and dressed. She also seemed about ready to leave the house, no doubt to take care of those pesky Saturday errands. If only that were all *she* had to worry about, Reine thought, greeting the tall, too-thin woman who'd worked for her uncle for as long as she could remember. And while Nora politely invited them inside, she couldn't keep her startled, bespectacled gaze from Cash.

Staring at him, she asked Reine, "Did your uncle tell you to see me about something?"

"No, and I'm afraid Uncle Jasper wouldn't approve of our being here, either. But this is really important, Nora."

"Sit, then."

They followed her into the sparsely furnished living room, with its identical heavy wooden benches made minimally comfortable by the addition of cushions. She and Cash sat opposite her uncle's assistant, who nearly faded into herself when she crossed her legs and hunched her shoulders forward.

"It's about Gray," Reine began.

Nora's painfully thin features pinched together. "I heard he'd disappeared...so I guess he still hasn't turned up, right?"

"That's because he's been kidnapped," Cash told her.

Nora's gray eyes grew large behind her glasses. "Mr. Matlock didn't say a thing."

"He was told not to," Reine explained. "The problem is, the kidnappers want a lot of money, and if Uncle Jasper can't come up with it... Well, I'm afraid for Gray."

She wasn't about to tell the woman he had no intentions of even trying. Surely, panic had been talking. He'd probably already changed his mind.

"So why come to me?"

"For information," Cash said, "about any particular business rivals who may have seemed threatening toward Matlock over the past few months."

"You mean other than yourself?" she sniped, sitting tall, her loyalty to her employer evident. "No one else, to my knowledge."

"Are you certain?" Reine asked. "Think hard,

Nora. This could be important. We're trying to figure out who might be responsible before—''

"It could mean my brother's life," Cash said.

Which made Reine gape. Cash calling Gray his "brother" was certainly a first.

Nora seemed even more surprised. "'Brother'?"

"Jasper Matlock is my biological father."

The woman blinked several times as if digesting that news, then quickly gathered herself together.

"Mr. Matlock has had lot of disagreements lately. You know, worries over the business and all. I thought maybe he was going to take that offer from Evan Bixler, but—"

"What about Evan Bixler?" Reine interrupted, remembering Cash had mentioned the man as being one of her uncle's chief competitors. "What sort of offer?"

Nora twitched and hunched inward again, obviously undecided about explaining.

"Please," Reine said. "I swear to you, this is for Gray, no other reason."

Slowly, she nodded. "Mr. Bixler wanted to buy into Matlock Construction. He would have provided the necessary capital to get the company back on its feet. Your uncle didn't want anything to do with him. Said something about shady business practices and how he wouldn't front for a hoodlum."

"A 'hoodlum'?" Cash echoed. "He used that exact word?"

"That he did. He kind of surprised me, but your fa— Uh, Mr. Matlock doesn't like his decisions questioned, so I just listened while he talked."

"How long ago did Bixler make the offer?"

"Two, maybe three weeks. I don't remember the

exact day.'' Nora looked anxiously from one to the other. ''Do you think Mr. Bixler was so angry about being turned down that he might have done it?''

''We don't know what to think yet,'' Reine said. ''We're trying to sort it all out.''

''I wish I could be of more help. I would hate to see anything happen to Grayson.''

''One more thing,'' Cash said. ''Does the name Selena Cullen mean anything to you?''

''S-Selena Cullen?'' Nora stammered and began blinking rapidly again. ''You know about her?''

Her heart sinking, Reine met Cash's gaze. So there was more to the story, after all. But Nora wouldn't give them details, even upon prompting.

So they thanked her profusely, asked her to keep their visit to herself, and left.

They were on their way back to the truck stop and her car when Reine said, ''I wonder what exactly Uncle Jasper meant by Bixler's being a hoodlum.''

She didn't even want to think about Selena Cullen, let alone talk about her.

''Or if he even had room to criticize,'' Cash said. ''He does have a tendency to get fixated on certain ideas that aren't fact. So that's the first thing I want to establish.''

''But how do we find out?''

''Let a professional do it.''

''The sheriff?''

She wasn't entirely opposed to the idea. Maybe it was time to go against her uncle's wishes on this one.

''I meant private investigator. Don't worry, I already know of a firm.''

''A good one, I hope.''

"Steven Kessler & Associates in Santa Fe. I only use the best."

Reine would expect no less of him, and yet...

She asked, "Why did you need to hire a private investigator?"

"You don't want to know."

Probably not. Undoubtedly it had to do with some takeover plan or other, maybe even of Matlock Construction. Already worrying about the unknown deadline, however, she was glad Cash already had an in.

"How fast does this company work?"

"We should have a dossier on Evan Bixler by tonight. And while I'm at it, I'll see what they can find out about Selena Cullen and her whereabouts."

Thankfully, he didn't elaborate.

Cash pulled into the truck stop's parking lot and stopped at her car.

"You know, I really have to check on Aunt Marlene," Reine said.

"That's fine. I need to catch up on some business with Nemesio."

"Then I guess I'll see you later. So when do we rendezvous?"

Giving her one of those looks that made her squirm inside, Cash said, "That's up to you, isn't it."

"If you're not going to be serious—"

"Don't worry," he interrupted. "I'll find you."

She nodded and left the pickup, a growing sense of unease filling her at the thought of facing Aunt Marlene with unanswered questions about Selena Cullen.

Chapter Eight

Work was already in progress on the new house when Cash arrived at the pueblo. The eight-inch-high concrete-block stem wall—elevated to avert erosion caused by rain—had already been poured the week before. A small but dedicated crew including the owner, his wife and the older of their sons, was hard at work setting the oversize adobe bricks in place and applying mortar with short-handled shovels.

Spotting Nemesio working on the area above what would be one of the doorways, Cash waved a guy off and climbed up his ladder. Cash's frustration over Gray's disappearance was enough to make him doubt himself. He needed the physical labor to ground him, to make him stronger.

And he needed to make certain Nemesio Escobar hadn't been involved.

His uncle was just about to lay the second angle iron above the lintel when Cash got to the top of the ladder and grabbed the other end. They set the bar in together as they'd done so many times in the past.

"Uncle, I need a favor."

His expression neutral, Nemesio said, "So ask."

"You might not like it."

"There's a lotta things in life I don't like, but you know I'd do anything for you or Luna."

They were the only family Nemesio had, and Cash knew he'd lay down his life for them if it came to that. But would his uncle do something illegal? Something that would hurt someone else he cared about?

The uncertainty had bothered him while he'd been trying to fall asleep the night before. First, possibilities involving Selena Cullen had gone around and around in his mind. Then others involving his uncle had surfaced, as well. He couldn't forget the weird argument between Nemesio and his mother.

"So what is it you need, Cash?"

"Help me find Gray."

"You're right." A frown narrowed his uncle's broad face. "I don't like it."

"But you'll do it? For me?"

Nemesio busied himself laying small adobe-veneer bricks on either side of the angle irons.

"Why can't you leave it alone?" he muttered darkly. "Don't involve yourself. Leave it up to fate and his own kind."

"I am involved because I am his kind, Uncle, as much as I'm yours. Mom was right about that."

His uncle looked up from his work to meet Cash's steady gaze. "But you turned your back on him. You chose sides and never wavered."

"But I shouldn't have had to choose. And it wasn't because of anything Gray did, but because of who our father was."

"Your father was Zane Abreu, a good man who loved your mother and you!"

He had no argument there. "Matlock's being my

father is a biological fact, but not one that makes me sentimental toward him, if that's your worry. But about Gray…''

When Nemesio abruptly quit his work and descended the ladder, Cash followed suit.

He'd been forced to walk away from everything he'd known or cared about on the land where he'd been raised—especially Gray and Reine. The alternative—acceptance of something that would have been a daily insult to his mother—had been unthinkable.

And Nemesio was wrong about his not wavering. He'd done so hundreds of times, especially at the beginning, when he'd been young and full of dreams.

He'd wished he could reclaim them both—the best friend who was really his brother, and the girl he loved. But Jasper Matlock had been Gray's father in truth and might as well have been Reine's. Jasper had taken in his wife's niece as his own, even though he'd so easily tossed away the product of his union with a woman who wasn't his own kind.

"What makes you think I can find Gray when the tracks were purposely obliterated?" Nemesio asked, the moment his feet touched solid ground.

Cash started. He hadn't heard anyone mention that before. The supposition had been that the kidnapper cleverly had used the river to confuse anyone who might follow them. So why did his uncle think otherwise?

Think or *know?*

Words stuck in his throat and he had to make a special effort to release them.

"I was figuring you could ask around, spread the word through all the pueblos in this area, maybe pick up some information about anyone acting suspicious. Surely there's been some speculation already.''

After all, pueblos were small communities not immune to gossip.

Nemesio didn't respond, however, and Cash's already troubled heart grew even heavier.

''You don't want Gray found, do you, Uncle?''

''Why should I care when he will soon have everything that should be yours as the firstborn?''

Normally endowed with a calm, even introspective nature, Nemesio was bristling with anger, his ruddy face dark. Cash could only remember seeing him so angry once before, when Cash had arrived at the pueblo bruised and bloodied after Matlock's beating. His uncle had been ready to declare war against the man who'd done this to a member of his family. Cash had had to convince Nemesio that going after Matlock in return would only get his father fired and both parents banished from the spread, as he already had been.

Having thought about the land a lot the night before, Cash said, ''Matlock wouldn't even own half of that spread if he hadn't married Marlene. It's Gray's birthright, not mine.''

''Then why are you so damn set on owning it?''

''Because I can! And because I vowed I would.''

''Because the bastard sold you and your mother off to his foreman like so much chattel when he thought you might hinder his plans?''

''I won't deny it.''

Though he *would* deny that revenge was sweet. It always seemed to leave a bitter taste in his mouth.

And in truth, both he and his mother had been

better off with Zane Abreu than they ever would have been with Jasper Matlock, himself.

"Hey, Nemesio!" called the owner-to-be of the new house. "We need your opinion over here."

Without another word, his uncle went to see what the man wanted, leaving Cash with his own thoughts.

If he took the land from Matlock, it would be the same as stealing his brother's birthright. While Cash didn't care about the land itself—only about owning what it represented—he knew it meant everything to Gray; that it had been the source of his identity even when they'd been small boys.

The thought might not have bothered Cash so much before, but suddenly everything had changed.

He only prayed that his uncle hadn't been the catalyst.

THE FIRST THING REINE noticed about her aunt when she walked into the dayroom was that she appeared calm, even relaxed. Stretched out on a pale cream-and-peach-chintz-covered chaise longue that matched the love seat and the curtains at the window, Aunt Marlene was perusing a magazine as if she didn't have a trouble in the world.

Reine put the change in humor to a good night's sleep and yet found no comfort in the supposition. Not after the message her aunt had left her.

Something was wrong.

"Aunt Marlene, I'm sorry I couldn't get here earlier."

"I'm so glad you're here now, Reine," Marlene said, setting down her magazine and removing her reading glasses, "so I can share the good news with you. Everything is going to be all right."

Reine's spirits soared. "Uncle Jasper made arrangements with the kidnapper, then? Is Gray here already?"

Marlene's smile tightened as she got to her feet. "Gray is not returned as of yet. And Jasper hasn't done anything as far as I know. I've taken charge of the situation myself."

"What do you mean…'yourself'? You notified the authorities?"

That was something she'd been hoping for since Gray had disappeared.

"No. Better than that. I paid Sam Valdez a visit this morning."

Reine frowned. "Valdez?"

"Don't sound so surprised. He and I were…close friends in the past. He's agreed to help me."

"How?"

"By getting me the money to save Gray, of course," her aunt said, as if she were dim-witted.

Which, in a way, Reine was feeling.

Aunt Marlene and Sam Valdez "close"? Reine wanted no further explanation, yet she had a healthy enough imagination. Close when? Surely before she'd married Uncle Jasper. That had been such a long time ago. Thirty-five years.

"And Valdez is going to give you two million dollars? Just like that?"

"In exchange for the land along the river, yes."

Gasping, Reine asked, "Uncle Jasper agreed to this?"

"That's the beautiful part—he doesn't have to."

Marlene sounded oddly triumphant and Reine recognized an unnatural sparkle in her eyes. She listened in amazement and dismay as her aunt revealed her plan.

The word *divorce* echoed in her mind as she said, "Surely it can't be that easy."

"Why ever not?"

She hated her aunt's flippant tone.

"Where are these papers your father had drawn up?" Reine demanded, wanting to see them for herself.

"My lawyer has them, of course." Marlene sounded annoyed with her. "I put in a call to him, but he hasn't gotten back to me yet." Pacing the length of the room, she said, "It is Saturday, but I'm certain I'll be hearing from him soon. I must. I need that money by Monday sunset."

Monday.

Sunset.

A little more than forty-eight hours from now.

Enough time for her and Cash to track down the kidnapper? Reine wondered. And if she convinced Aunt Marlene that they could, then didn't come through…

Tactfully, she said, "Aunt Marlene, surely you're not really going to start divorce proceedings when you're under such stress."

"I'm going to be prepared. Jasper has had enough time to sober up and think about—"

"So you've already told him?"

"No, not yet. He was gone when I got back to the house a while ago." Marlene's arms slid around her middle and she stopped before a window. "But as soon as he walks through that door…"

Tears stung the backs of Reine's eyelids as her

world crumbled a little more. Bit by bit, the family she'd come to think of as her own was falling apart.

Jasper Matlock didn't take ultimatums well. She could hardly believe Marlene was going to give him one.

But the poor woman was desperate. At her breaking point. She simply wasn't thinking straight or she wouldn't have gone to a quarrelsome neighbor—albeit a formerly "close friend"—over her husband.

"Aunt Marlene, you don't want to do this. You don't want to divorce Uncle Jasper."

"You're right." Her aunt faced her. "I don't. But I will if Jasper forces me. He thinks he can control everything, just as Papa did. Well, his willing Gray safe won't make it so. I love the land, too, but it's nothing to me when compared to my son. But Jasper—he'd do anything to keep from losing it, even convince himself that Gray is safe because Cash is the one who has him."

"That's ridiculous! Cash is helping me try to find out who might be responsible!"

Marlene took a deep breath and squeezed her eyes shut for a moment. "He's coming through for Gray, after all," she murmured. "I should have known he would."

"I'll tell Uncle Jasper—"

"What good would that do? He'd only say Cash is trying to establish his innocence or some such."

Undoubtedly her aunt was right.

That made learning the truth all the more imperative. Reine needed to find Cash right away and tell him....

What?

That the woman who'd inadvertently stolen his father from his mother was about to dump the man? Would Cash care? It might even give him cause to drag his heels a little.

So she wouldn't tell him. Not about the possible divorce. Not about Sam Valdez.

Not now.

If they could only foil Gray's kidnapper, Cash would never have to know.

A CALL TO HACIENDA Abreu put Reine in the direction of the pueblo where Nemesio Escobar still made his home. The young maid Gloria had said something about Cash's building a house, and she'd tried to envision him doing so literally.

How ridiculous. That would ruin his expensive manicure.

But, indeed, upon alighting from her car at the site half a mile down the road from the plaza, she spotted him on a ladder, hard at work applying mortar to the adobe bricks. She stood and stared, somewhat amazed.

"Is Cash expecting you?" asked a familiar woman's voice from behind.

Reine turned to face Cash's mother. "Luna, hello." Her first instinct was to envelop the older woman in a quick hug, but, not knowing how it would be received, she held herself back. "Cash *is* expecting to see me," she said, "but not here. I, uh, finished what I had to do faster than I'd thought and figured I'd play catch-up, save him some time. I didn't expect to find him hard at work." Curious, she turned back to watch. "I'm amazed he still remembers the trade."

"That's because he never gave it up completely.

He not only donates the materials for these projects, but himself.''

''What projects?''

''Helping people who can't otherwise afford their own homes to build one. It's a community effort. People helping each other with whatever skills they have. And then the work is returned on the coming projects, of course.''

''Kind of like the Habitat for Humanity program.''

''A similar principle,'' Luna agreed.

Reine was amazed. Of all the things she'd called Cash in her mind, ''benefactor'' had not been among them. This was a new and unexpected side of the man. One he apparently hid from the world.

And one that she liked. A lot.

It was then that Cash spotted her. ''Reine! Be down in a little while!'' he yelled.

She waved in response.

Watching Cash work fascinated her. His white T-shirt was streaked with reddish-brown earth as were his powerful arms. Even from a distance, she could see the flex and play of muscle as he lifted a shovelful of mortar and dumped it on top of the adobe brick.

''Would you like something cool to drink in the meantime?'' Luna asked, catching her attention. ''Iced tea?''

''That would be lovely.''

She followed Cash's mother to a couple of make-shift tables shaded by some big cottonwoods that stood behind one of the older houses in the community. Luna exchanged greetings with a pair of mud-covered workers who were taking their lunch break. A couple of kids grabbed some food from a second, heavily-laden table and ran off, laughing.

Two Pueblo women seemed to be in charge of the midday meal. The older one was making fry bread in a deep-sided, oil-filled black iron pan that sat on a single-burner hotplate. The other was using the fry bread to make Indian tacos with meat and cheese, shredded lettuce and salsa.

Reine's mouth began to water.

"If you're hungry," the fry-bread maker said, "help yourself."

"Thanks." Reine had her eye specifically on a platter heaped with homemade tamales, whose corn husks were tied in a way that she recognized. She chose one, peeled back the husk and took a bite. "Mmm, Luna, you still make the best tamales I've ever tasted."

"How do you know they're mine?"

"The way you tie them. And the taste. When we were kids, I always looked forward to Fridays, because I knew we'd all get some of your homemade tamales after school."

"That was so long ago...too long." Luna handed her a cup of the iced tea. "I told Cash turning his back on you and Gray was a mistake that he would live to regret, but he wouldn't listen to me."

Did he regret it? Reine wondered.

After washing down the last bite with a swig of the cool tea, she said, "He didn't have room in his heart for anything but making money so he could prove something, I guess. That he was as good as Uncle Jasper and could play on his field."

"There was that."

"What else?"

"Me. Cash felt he had to uphold my honor." Luna shook her head. "I told him that was ridiculous, that I had gotten over the bad feelings so many years before that I barely remembered them. But the pain was new to him, so I guess he couldn't understand. I had been infatuated with your uncle for a short while, but for eighteen years, I knew what real love was with my husband. My son's true father."

"Zane was a good man and a nice one."

Reine remembered how he used to tell her tall tales with such sincerity that she always at least half believed them, no matter how wild.

One of the Pueblo women held out an Indian taco, saying, "Would you like to try?"

Reine felt it wouldn't be polite to refuse. She smiled and thanked the woman, then, at the first bite, made audible sounds of ecstasy.

Both cooks smiled and laughed with her.

Luna had heaped a plate with food and now brought it to the table that was just being vacated.

"Come. Sit," she said.

Reine placed her taco on a paper plate and added two more tamales and some fresh fruit. Then she joined Cash's mother. The women ate in companionable silence for a few moments before Luna spoke.

"Zane Abreu was everything Jasper Matlock wasn't," she told Reine. "They say behavior is learned, but Zane would never have approved of some of the things our son has done. He believed in love, not in vengeance."

"They also say the best revenge is living well," Reine said. "Cash certainly has mastered that art to a fault. Too bad he didn't stop there. Too bad he felt it necessary to cut himself off from Gray and me."

"It wasn't because he didn't love you both enough. I always thought that with time, he'd change his mind."

"And now fate has stepped in and changed it for him. At least in Gray's case,"

"At least," Luna emphasized, putting a different spin on the words.

And giving Reine something to mull over.

When she'd cleaned her plate, she thought about getting yet another tamale, even though she was full. Looking toward the food table, however, she hesitated. Cash's uncle was there, and he was staring at *her*.

"I don't think your brother likes my being here," she murmured to Luna.

The older woman gave her brother a quick look. He glared, then took his plate and drink and walked in the other direction, deliberately snubbing them.

Luna shook her head. "Nemesio is all worked up because he knows Cash is worried about Gray and is determined to do something."

"Why should he care?"

"Again, for me."

"He's had years to get over it," Reine said, amazed. Ever since Zane Abreu had died, leaving that letter for Cash. "They both have."

"Once Nemesio sinks his teeth into something, he doesn't let go until he's chewed it up good first. He's never found a way to make Jasper Matlock suffer."

"Cash has been doing a good enough job for the both of them."

"Unfortunately. But that's another problem. I think Nemesio is finding it difficult that his position is reversed. Until a few years ago, he was the male head of our family, such as it was. He was my son's mentor, taught him a trade and guided him into manhood. Then Cash's hard work and investments started paying off and suddenly Nemesio found himself working for his own nephew. He always had his own ambitions, but he was never able to do more than earn an honest living. Now he has more, but because of Cash. It grates on him."

"He complains about your son's success?"

"No, he would never do that. But I know my brother," Luna said, her expression as worried as her tone. "Nemesio's frustrations have been building. I only worry about what he might do to soothe them."

"YOU MIGHT AS WELL WAIT for me in the garden where you can relax," Cash suggested.

Though he and Reine had driven their own vehicles, they'd arrived at his place at the same time. Reine had seemed to be wound up, all nerves. And at the moment, she was wandering around the living room aimlessly.

"Isn't there anything useful I can do while you shower?" she asked.

To relieve the tension, he purposely said, "Scrub my back?"

But she didn't turn into the blushing beauty he loved to tease. The flashing of her eyes told him clearly how much he'd annoyed her.

"I was thinking more along the lines of calling your hotshot private investigator to see if he came up with anything."

"I already did that. I called from the truck and spoke to Steven directly."

He'd also picked up his messages, but hadn't yet

gotten back to a business associate who'd left him half a dozen and was making him real nervous. He meant to place a return call as soon as he got Reine out of the way.

"And?" she asked. "What did he learn?"

"Nothing on Selena Cullen yet. Evan Bixler's another story."

"Long version short," she requested.

"Bixler has certain friends the government doesn't exactly approve of."

"Which government?"

"The feds. These friends are into selling illegal product at high gain and Bixler is a suspect."

"Of drug trafficking?"

"Of money laundering," Cash clarified. "He seems to have more money than his businesses suggest he can make from them. And he keeps diversifying, buying new ones."

"So that's why he made that bid on Matlock Construction. What's our plan?"

"At the moment, Steven Kessler is having his best investigator shadow Bixler."

"I mean for us."

"I haven't decided yet." Getting impatient, Cash started toward the gallery, saying, "If you're hungry, the kitchen is that way."

"After all that food I ate at the pueblo? You must be kidding. But everything was spicy, so I could use something to drink."

"Help yourself."

Still seeming distracted, Reine finally left him alone and Cash detoured straight into his office where he finally placed that call.

Once connected, he said, "So talk!" without any preamble.

"I need to see you," the man on the other end said. *"Now."*

He knew the what—Matlock Ranch—but not the why.

"Sounds urgent."

"In person!"

Cash thought quickly. He'd have to get away from Reine without arousing her suspicions. And then he would settle this matter once and for all.

"All right," he agreed. "I've got to clean up, but I'll meet you at your place in an hour."

"The sooner the better."

After hanging up, Cash called Steven Kessler & Associates and lucked into the excuse he needed to ditch Reine for a while. He headed for the kitchen, which took up nearly one whole side of the house. He'd built it inside/outside, to be open to the court-yard and the oversize brick grill, which Reine was inspecting.

"We cook all our meats out here," he told her.

"A side of beef at a time?"

"Only when we have guests."

Pirouetting to take in the garden, she wistfully said, "Talk about kitchens I'd like to spend time in...."

"That can be arranged."

For a brief moment, he visualized her happy laughter ringing through the large room as she learned to cook traditional dishes from his mother.

Then he remembered why he'd set out to find her in the first place. "I just talked to Kessler. It seems that Selena Cullen has finally turned up."

"Where?"

"Enchanted. I figured we'd pay her a visit."

She gave him a once-over. "You want to go looking like that?"

"What? You don't think she'd appreciate the construction-worker aspect?" Cash had a feeling that Reine did, considering the way she'd been watching him on site. "I'm about to jump in the shower now," he said. "Since we have to go back to Santa Fe anyway, why don't I meet you at your place in a couple of hours."

"Why so long? What if she leaves?"

"I need to take care of some business," he hedged. Not exactly a lie. "Besides, Kessler has someone tailing the Cullen woman, too. We'll know where to find her wherever she might go. And you could probably use a short lie-down."

"Probably," she agreed, already seeming distracted again as she reentered the kitchen. "But don't take too long."

Relieved by the ease with which he'd succeeded, Cash steered her toward the front door.

"Get some rest," he said. "We don't know what we might be getting ourselves into."

Which went double for him.

Chapter Nine

Sam Valdez let Cash in, barking, "About time you got here, Abreu!"

He'd taken less than the anticipated hour, but Valdez appeared ready to jump out of his skin as he stalked into the living room. All those phone messages should have clued him in to how anxious Valdez was. Following him, Cash threw himself into a cowhide-covered chair in what was undeniably a man's room. Valdez's idea of decorating was turning an old beat-up boot into a planter for some scrawny cactus.

Valdez poured himself a whiskey from the elaborate bar on the opposite side of the room. "Want one?"

"Too early to drink," Cash said, suddenly becoming impatient himself. "What's so all-fired important that you had to see me right away?"

Dashing down the whiskey, the rancher grimaced as he swallowed. "Everything's falling into place for us, Abreu. *She* came to me and made me an offer—"

"Who?"

"Marlene Matlock."

Startled, Cash sat up straighter. "What did she want?"

"I get her the money for her son...she gets me the land along the river."

Cash wondered if Marlene had bothered mentioning this to her niece since Reine hadn't said a thing about it. Then again, he'd barely spoken to Reine before rushing her off so he could get himself over here. Maybe that was why she'd been acting so weird. Not that he could ask her about it....

"How can Marlene guarantee you anything?" he asked Valdez. "Last I knew, the old buzzard was refusing to do a damn thing to save Gray because he thought *I'd* snatched him."

"You?" Valdez guffawed. "If he really believes that, he's dumber than dirt."

"I think he has himself convinced, because the land's all he has left and he won't allow himself to think about parting with it."

"Ah, now here comes the sweet end of the deal. Marlene's papa set things up all nice and legal so she couldn't lose what shoulda belonged to *my* family in the first place. She and Jasper co-own the river property, but only for as long as they stay married. Some kinda business partnership or other." Valdez poured himself another drink. "And you'll love this—if old Jasper don't agree to sell, she's gonna give him the boot. Then the property reverts to her solely. So, any way you look at it, we're in a win-win situation!"

He tossed back another whiskey.

And Cash sat there, stunned. For years his goal had been to get the part of the spread along the river away from Matlock. He'd even made a pact with

Valdez about the water rights to enlist his aid. If Valdez could somehow get him the land, he'd have the water rights in pepetuity.

This was everything he could have hoped for and more, so why wasn't he happier?

As Valdez seemed to notice…

"I don't hear no fireworks, Abreu." He stalked across the room and stood over Cash. "What's goin' on in that head of yours?"

"I'm not sure about this."

"Not sure? Crissakes, man, this is what you been waitin' for!"

"Yes. But maybe Gray being in trouble has made me rethink my priorities."

Valdez's big hands curled into fists. "And maybe you've gone plumb *loco!*"

"That, too." *Why else would he drag his feet on this deal?*

"It wouldn't be that you been talkin' a big game without the chips to see it through, would it?"

"Two million's a lot of money," Cash agreed.

"More than you got?"

"I could scrape it together with some help."

He'd have to call in some favors, count on a couple of quick and highly unconventional loans against his business. He routinely reinvested what he didn't spend on keeping up his life-style, so it wasn't like he had the cash.

"But I need to think about this before I do anything," he said, more to himself than to Valdez.

The other man cursed a blue streak.

Cash wasn't moved.

"Time is in short commodity!" Valdez insisted. "Marlene says she needs the money on Monday."

Monday...

So now they had their time frame.

"We still have two days, then." Cash rose, practically going nose-to-nose with Valdez. Realizing the man wasn't too happy with him, and considering they'd had a deal of his own making, he tried to be reassuring. "Don't worry. Whatever I decide, you'll get what's coming to you."

"You can rest assured I will, Abreu. Because if you don't come through, I'll find myself another backer!"

"The hell you will!"

"I can't let Marlene down. She's counting on me."

Understanding slowly filling him, Cash stared. "You and Marlene...?"

"A long time ago, yeah. But she's the kinda woman, once she gets in a man's blood, she's there for good. You wouldn't understand unless you've been there."

He'd been there, all right, Cash thought ironically.

"If she meant so much to you," Cash said, asking the man exactly what he'd asked himself so many times, "why did you ever let her go?"

"Not my choice. First her papa took her from me. Then her own sense of loyalty, even though she'd found out about you and Luna. So, you wanna back down, you go ahead. You're not the only one with deep pockets in these parts."

"Don't start looking for that other partner too soon," Cash warned him.

"I'll give you until tomorrow morning to decide, Abreu. Then I go elsewhere."

Cash was already tuning him out as he headed for

the door. Things had just gotten more complicated than he'd ever imagined they could be.

Sam Valdez might be in a win-win situation. As for himself, he was in a real quandary.

Two million—he could manage it if he so chose.

He could have the final say in his battle with Jasper Matlock.

And at the same time, he could be responsible for setting Gray free; could be a hero of sorts.

Only...*what then?*

He'd own the only thing his brother cared about.

And the woman he'd determined to make his own would despise him for it.

On the other hand, if he didn't come through, Valdez would take in some stranger on the deal. He'd have his water rights. And Marlene would probably be so grateful he'd have her, too, one way or another.

But Gray would still be out the land.

And Cash wouldn't be able to live with himself, because there was that degree-of-separation theory to haunt him—if he hadn't gone after Matlock Construction and decimated it, the old man would have the means to buy his son back without worrying about losing the spread.

As far as Cash was concerned, morning was going to come too quickly for his comfort.

THE MORE REINE THOUGHT about it, the less sense it made to wait for Cash to get himself to Santa Fe before approaching Selena Cullen.

Who knew how long his business would tie him up?

Besides, as tired as she was, Reine didn't want a

lie-down. She wanted to feel as if she were doing something positive.

Something to help Gray.

Only how?

What approach would get her what she wanted? And what did she want other than to discern whether or not Selena Cullen was involved? If that was possible. And if the woman was guilty, she wouldn't actually come out and admit it. But maybe she could be shaken up a bit, Reine thought; made to feel reckless enough to let something slip.

As she approached Enchanted on foot, she looked around, wondering who was keeping an eye on the store. She saw a lot of tourists milling about, but no one who looked like a private investigator.

Of course, that would be the point....

Entering the gallery, she was relieved to find fewer tourists inside than she'd expected. Dominick was busy with a couple of customers—two middle-age women decked out in Santa Fe chic who were effusing over a display of kachinas. One woman was staring at the fireplace that now boasted a Sold sign, and a young couple was rifling through the handcrafted switch plates the salesman had taken such care to arrange just the night before.

Reine recognized Selena Cullen the moment she spotted the woman, the fiery dark hair being a dead giveaway. The color was more mahogany than a true red, but that and the high, broad cheekbones, snapping dark eyes and naturally bronzed skin revealed something of the woman's heritage. Despite the last name, Selena appeared to be mestizo like Cash—a mix of New Mexico's Anglo, Hispanic and Native American cultures.

The gallery owner busied herself straightening a display of prints on one wall.

Her pulse thrumming now that she was about to stick out her neck, Reine drew closer. She only hoped there was no way she could worsen the situation.

Selena turned to catch her staring, and with a broad smile, asked, "Can I help you?"

"I hope so. My name is Reine Kendrick—"

The smile instantly vanished. "What is it you want from me?"

It was the same reaction she'd gotten from the manager of Green Chiles. Obviously, Dolores Zaldava had found a way to forewarn her friend.

"Could we talk someplace private?" Reine asked.

She thought Selena was going to say no, but, in the end, the gallery owner gave in grudgingly, the sharp tilt of her head toward the back of the store indicating that Reine should follow her.

They cut through a rear office and storage room and came out onto a small patio ringed with aspens, whose center was Saltillo-tiled and furnished with a wrought-iron table and chairs. Two half-empty coffee cups and an ashtray holding a crushed cigar whose heavy scent still hung in the air told Reine the area had been recently in use.

Resting a hip against the table, Selena folded her arms over her chest. "All right. You have your privacy."

Praying that she would do this right, Reine said, "First let me tell you how sorry I am about your son's death."

"Leave Jimmy out of this!" the woman snapped, her dark eyes instantly bright with unshed tears.

"What do you want from me?" she asked again. "Did Jasper send you?"

"No. My uncle doesn't know I'm here."

"Then why are you?"

"I'm here for myself...and for my aunt. You and she have a lot in common."

"You mean your uncle?"

Trying to ignore the implication, Reine swallowed hard and stayed on the same track. "You both suffered a loss having to do with a son, although I'm hoping for a better ending for my cousin than your poor Jimmy had."

"Your cousin?" Selena echoed as if she didn't know who Reine meant.

"Grayson Matlock."

"Ah, Jasper's precious son."

Selena's seeming perplexity instantly cleared, making Reine wonder if she had a talent for lying.

"He's missing," Reine said. "Kidnapped, actually. Aunt Marlene is beside herself. She's terrified that something will happen to Gray...as am I."

All the while she spoke, Reine watched Selena for a reaction that didn't come. No break in her expression. Not even in her posture. Surely any mother who'd just lost a son would at least flinch...if she had nothing to hide.

Instead, Selena calmly challenged her: "So why are you here?"

"You understand the loss and grief only a mother can know," Reine continued, trying to get Selena to identify with Aunt Marlene. "And if I or my aunt could give you back your son, we would."

Selena blinked, and a thread of understanding passed between them.

"You suspect *I* had something to do with this kidnapping?"

"Did you?"

Selena laughed, the sound unnatural. "Jasper *did* send you, didn't he?"

"No."

"His guilt has finally caught up to him."

So she did blame him for Jimmy's suicide.

"Taking over your son's company was a business deal."

"Really? And was Jasper's seducing me into telling him everything about Jimmy's financial difficulties part of his business policy, as well?"

Reine couldn't think how to respond to that. She'd suspected her uncle had been unfaithful, but not like this. Not using an affair—sex—to further his profits.

"Shocked?" Selena asked. "How do you think I felt when your uncle dropped me the moment he got what he really wanted? He used me. I was just another stepping-stone...a temporary possession...a means to an end. Only, who could have predicted what kind of end for my son?"

Reine's mouth was dry when she said, "I'm sure that never occurred to Uncle Jasper."

"So you want me to what? Feel sorry for him because *his* son is missing?" Selena laughed again—a kind of controlled hysteria. "Maybe Gray got sick of him and disappeared on purpose. He could show up at any time. Right? but me...I'll never see *my* son again. I will live with that anguish every minute of every day of my life. I hope Jasper suffers every bit as much as I have, and you can tell him I said so when you see him!"

The woman was so hostile that Reine felt she had

no choice but to leave—and to wonder if she hadn't made a mess of things, after all.

"I'VE BEEN DOING SOME thinking," Reine said as Cash drove them down the highway back to Española. "I never should have listened to Uncle Jasper when he refused to consider outside help, but I didn't feel that it was my decision to make. We should have brought in the sheriff in the first place. Maybe we still should."

"That is an option," Cash said cautiously, "though I don't know that it makes sense to interfere with the forces that have already been set in motion."

"It's just that we—*I* have handled this all wrong from the get-go."

Though Cash was less than thrilled that Reine had gone off on her own to face Selena Cullen, he hadn't given her a hard time about it. She was already beating herself up over the meeting for nothing. Who was to say the two of them together could have gotten anything more revealing out of the woman than Reine had by herself.

And if Reine had set the Cullen woman into motion, one of Kessler's operatives would be right behind her and would keep them posted.

Meanwhile, Cash was on a mission. Determined to track down the last of their leads before deciding what to do about the money, he was preparing himself to face Evan Bixler.

Pulling off the highway, he thought about his deal with Sam Valdez and his doubts about pursuing it. That he couldn't discuss his conflicted state with

Reine had him on edge, but he wasn't willing to confirm her suspicions.

Reine already thought she knew the worst about him, but he feared she hadn't scratched the surface of who he really was.

"The pachucos are out, showing off," she said as they drove into Española, which proudly hailed itself the Low Rider Capital of the World.

Cars—ten, twenty, thirty years old and more—were kept in pristine condition by members of the low-rider clubs, which were composed typically of young Latino men. On weekend evenings, the shining vehicles—their metal panels painted with intricate murals, their chassis fitted with unusual hydraulics—paraded slowly around the streets, their undercarriages low to the ground.

Cash came to a stop behind a purple-and-green Thunderbird; its elaborate mural displayed a bald eagle whose wings were spread across the trunk. Without warning, the rear end of the car bucked nearly three feet off the ground as if the driver were trying to launch the big bird. When the car fell back down, its bottom scraped the pavement with an impressive and purposeful shower of sparks.

Horns honked and pedestrians whistled and applauded in appreciation.

"Not bad," Cash murmured.

"I'm surprised you don't own one of those babies."

He grinned at her. "Who said I don't?"

Traffic was moving again. He checked addresses. A block along, he turned right. They didn't go very far before he spotted the establishment Steven Kessler had told him about. The large parking lot behind

The Bix Box was nearly full, and a low rider was cruising the aisles, a handful of admirers gathering around to watch.

"Looks like this is a hangout for one of the low-rider clubs," Reine said.

Cash parked at the far end of the lot, away from the action. On their way to the bar's entrance, they passed several more brightly painted vehicles.

"I doubt Evan Bixler will tell us anything more than Selena Cullen did," Reine said. "And he's a lot more dangerous."

"Don't worry. I'm not going to be making any accusations. We'll keep this friendly."

"Then what are you going to talk to him about?"

"The plan is to approach him as one businessman to another," Cash replied.

But once inside, he wondered how big a challenge that might present. The interior was dark, smoke-filled and, above all, noisy. A televised sporting event was competing with Latino music and a cacophony of voices.

The bartender was a young Latina of considerable charm. She wore skintight jeans and a T-shirt with Don't Touch printed across her chest.

"Two drafts," Cash said as he pulled out a couple of stools.

"Coming up."

When she delivered the beers, he not only paid but gave the comely bartender an extra twenty. "Tell your boss I'm looking for him. Name's Cash Abreu."

"What if Mr. Bixler isn't in?"

"He'll be in."

Sticking the tip in a back pocket, she shrugged and moved off, presumably to find Bixler.

"I thought you'd never met the man," Reine said, turning her stool so she was facing him.

"I haven't. But he'll know who I am."

"Living dangerously," she murmured as she was shoved up against him by a couple of guys who were roughhousing their way out of the bar.

There were dangers…and dangers, Cash thought, his hands on her arms, setting her back on her stool.

He'd suggested she let her hair down and she had done so. Literally. Thick golden-blond strands curled around her shoulders. And while she was still wearing a skirt, she'd paired it with a soft pullover that exposed her long neck and delicate collarbones. She'd always been sensitive there. He imagined she still was.

He was giving his imagination free rein when the bartender returned to her station.

"Up there." She pointed to a second-floor loft area accessible by a single staircase.

Reine was already on her feet, her beer forgotten. Cash took a swig, then set his mug down on the bar next to hers before placing a hand at the small of her back and moving toward the stairs.

She leaned into him long enough to say, "I hope you know what you're doing."

"So do I."

When they reached the second floor, the noise had lowered a level. A quick glance around the half-dozen tables and Cash identified Bixler immediately. He sat alone, a half-empty bottle of tequila before him, a cloud of cigar smoke around his head. Balding and unassuming in stature, he would disappear into a crowd.

Not so the two muscular guys at the next table, who silently followed their approach.

"Cash Abreu, we meet at last," Bixler said without removing his cigar. "I'm a big fan. Pull up a chair for your lady and sit."

While Cash did so, Bixler waved to get the waitress's attention. He held up his shot glass and two fingers. Then he centered his attention on Cash.

"So what do you think of my place?"

"That it's surprisingly out of your normal sphere."

"A man needs to kick back once in a while. I like doing it where I can call the shots. You ought to try it," Bixler said, just as the waitress came by with the glasses. "Thanks, honey." He filled them and pushed one toward each of them. "To your continued good health—both of you."

Reacting to the health implication, Cash locked gazes with Reine. Her eyes widened and her mouth dropped open slightly. He raised his glass in salute; she did the same. They tossed back the tequila together.

Laughing, Bixler slammed his palm onto the tabletop. "That's what I like. A woman who's all woman but isn't afraid of a challenge."

"You are an unusual man, Mr. Bixler," she said.

"Call me Bix, sweetheart. Call me anytime you want." The man laughed at his own joke, but when no one joined him, he quickly sobered and got down to business. "What is it you think I can do for you, Cash?"

"I thought I might do something for you in the way of a business proposition."

"All depends. What business?"

"Matlock Construction."

Bixler puffed on his cigar. "Go on."

"Jasper Matlock is at a particularly low point right now, both financially and personally. He might be in the mood to sell."

"That'd be interesting," Bixler said, setting his cigar in the ashtray, "If I was in the mood to buy."

"My sources tell me you recently made him an offer, and that you weren't too happy when he refused."

"Moods change."

Cash kept pushing. "So what *does* interest you at the moment?"

"Your real reason for coming to see me. You don't need a partner."

"Not financially."

"Then what's the point?"

"I'm not Jasper Matlock's favorite person."

"No, but you are his son."

That statement startled Cash.

"One of them," he agreed. "The *wrong* one. I have even more reason to want some…let's call it 'satisfaction'…from Matlock than you do."

Bixler sat back, eyes narrowing. "'Satisfaction' is an interesting concept."

"Some people will do anything to get it. How about you, Bix?"

"I do what's necessary to uphold my reputation."

"Just what kind of a reputation do you have?" Reine asked.

"The ladies don't complain."

"I meant your business competitors."

"Ooh, she's smart, too." Bixler's gaze on her intensified. "As for myself, I prefer smart women, but I hear Jasper Matlock's not especially fond of them. Is that why you and your uncle are always at odds?"

Realizing Bixler somehow knew who Reine was without having been introduced, Cash remained passive only by sheer will. "You know an awful lot about both of us," he said. "Certainly more than I do about you."

"Kind of makes you think you'd never want to run up against me, doesn't it?"

That sounded like a threat. Cash wondered if they could actually be on to something here.

"I can hold my own."

"Good for you." Bixler grabbed his cigar from the ashtray. "Now, if we're done…"

"Then I take it you're not interested in a deal," Cash said, pushing just a tad further.

"I think I'd rather get satisfaction in my own way. It'll taste that much sweeter."

While Cash was ready to stick it out—to force Bixler into some kind of admission—Reine was tugging at his arm, her voice strained as she said, "Then we'll leave you to the rest of your bottle."

The man was already ignoring them and concentrating on relighting his cigar.

As they left the table, Cash noticed the two bodyguards were gone. They'd somehow slipped away without his ever noticing. He kept his gaze roaming as they descended the stairs and pushed through the crowd to the door, but he didn't spot them.

Something didn't feel right….

The moment they hit fresh air, Reine asked, "Are you as spooked as I am?"

"Maybe more."

Cash kept his gaze moving over their surroundings. Not that he could see much in the dark—Bixler didn't waste any electricity on his parking lot. Still, the moon was full and a handful of people crowded around a spiffy '64 Impala parked near the entrance of the lot.

"Bixler's finding out about you wouldn't be so hard," Cash mused aloud as they headed for the Jaguar, "but me?"

"Nora Archer didn't even know, and she's been working for Uncle Jasper for longer than I can remember. He doesn't exactly go around advertising it."

"And neither do I. Bixler must have done some serious digging," Cash concluded.

The Jaguar was in sight when another low rider—a '74 Monte Carlo—crept around a row of cars. The fancy paint job seemed to glow in the moonlight. Even at a distance Cash got a glimpse of an Aztec pyramid on the hood.

A noise to his right made him whip around, pushing Reine behind him where he could protect her, if necessary.

"What is it?"

He caught a flash of movement behind some cars—someone skulking around, watching them?

"I don't know," he said in a low voice, "but I'm going to find out. Stay here."

"Cash!" she hissed after him.

But he was already flying between two cars, using them to propel himself to the other side. By the time he popped into the open, it was for naught. Nothing. He ran past several cars, checking between them, but whatever he'd seen had vanished.

"False alarm," he called, even as he heard the squeal of brakes.

Cash flew around just in time to behold the "Aztec Pyramid" about to make a sacrifice of Reine!

Chapter Ten

The low rider whacked down so close to Reine and with such force that she stumbled. Sparks showered over her as she flew forward, landing hard on her knees.

Her pulse thundering from the scare, she shouted, "What the hell do you think you're doing!"

In response, the driver revved his engine and aimed the nose of his vehicle straight at her.

For a split second, she was mesmerized by the headlights.

"Reine!" Cash yelled. "Duck between the cars!"

But she couldn't act fast enough, though she was already getting to her feet.

There was only one recourse open to her.

She launched herself forward, landed flat on the car's hood, nose first into the tinted windshield. Her glimpse of the driver ceased when he slammed on the brakes and she slipped away from him.

Frantic, Reine grasped at a windshield wiper, which immediately activated. At the same time, she felt the car's hydraulics grind into action.

"Let go!" Cash yelled.

But she was stuck, with the material of her sleeve

caught on the windshield wiper that was still functioning. She fought to free herself. Her legs flew out into midair, her skirts whipping around her like some kind of sail. The fabric of her sleeve ripped even as the front end of the car bucked and plummeted, taking her stomach along with it.

Then Reine hurtled off the car's hood, while the fireworks caused by the undercarriage hitting pavement celebrated her slow-motion flight.

She slammed into what felt like a wall, which immediately collapsed under the force of the collision.

Cash grunted as they hit the ground together, then managed to ask, "Are you all right?"

Sprawled over him, she took a shaky breath and tried regaining use of her limbs. "I think so."

He was instantly on his feet, taking her with him. Seeming about to go after the vehicle, he stopped when another low rider turned down the aisle and drew alongside the first. Bright lights flashed on, pinning them in their glare.

"Let's get out of here!"

Cash hooked an arm around Reine's waist and pulled her with him toward the Jaguar.

Reine stumbled, her feet missing the ground a few times as he propelled her faster and faster. She managed a glance behind them. The headlights seemed to be closing in on them, and the other low rider's taillights glowed a brilliant red. That car was now backing up toward them, as well.

Her pulse jagged and she croaked, "They're both coming after us!"

Cash responded instantly, and with a burst of speed, in a matter of seconds had her at the Jaguar.

He tore open the passenger door. Rather than stuffing her inside as she'd expected, Cash went for the glove compartment where he retrieved something.

Then he barked, "Get in!" and positioned himself like a shield, legs spread, gun aimed in a two-handed grip at their would-be attackers.

"They're stopping," Reine said even as she followed orders. "What if *they* have guns?"

"Close your door and open mine."

His weapon still aimed at two other vehicles, Cash was already moving around the nose of the Jaguar. He kept the car between him and the low riders.

Reine's heart pounded and she couldn't breathe easy until he was inside with his own door closed. He set the gun on the console, barrel pointed forward.

She peered through the rear window. The Monte Carlo had backed around the aisle so that, no matter which way they went, they would have to face one of the low riders.

"They're still there, waiting."

"Probably wondering what to do next," he said, starting up the engine. "Hang on!"

Cash didn't hesitate. The Jaguar not only flew out of the parking spot, but he propelled it straight back toward the headlights, which suddenly started moving away from them—fast.

"Look at him haul butt!" Reine said. "He's afraid you'll hit his precious car."

"Good."

The Jaguar stopped and, with Cash shifting fast, jumped forward and turned straight for the Monte Carlo.

"You're going to hit him!"

At the last minute, Cash swerved around the low

rider and ducked down another aisle. And Reine realized he'd been taking a calculated risk meant to
distract the driver.

Far ahead, at the other end, a second vehicle
crawled toward the entrance.

Reine didn't want to know how fast they were
going. She only prayed that no pedestrian stepped in
front of the speeding Jaguar.

Cash barely slowed to careen around the aisle end,
then catapulted them toward the entrance. The low
rider she'd spotted was already stopped directly in
their path to block their escape, painted skeletons
grinning out at them from the vehicle's side.

Her heart climbed into her throat as Cash accel-
erated and bore down on the clumsy car. Preparing
herself for impact, Reine prayed. She could hardly
believe her eyes when, at the last possible moment,
the other vehicle seemed to jump out of their path as
if it had been goosed.

And Cash shot them straight out of the lot and
back toward the main drag.

Reine took a shaky breath that seemed to ripple
down the entire length of her body. "Looks like we
finally pressed the wrong buttons."

"Or the right ones," Cash amended.

THE ONE THING CASH KNEW was that no way in hell
would he let Reine stay alone that night. And compared to her place, his was a fortress. So he took the
road east toward Chimayo rather than one that would
have taken them south to Santa Fe.

If Reine had any objections, she kept them to herself.

She was that scared.

As was Cash on her behalf. For a moment, he'd thought he would have to watch her die.

If anything had happened to her...

He steeled himself against the image. That hadn't happened. And if he had anything to say about it, it never would.

He kept watch in the rearview mirror, but caught no lights swing behind them. As far as he could tell, they were in the clear—for the moment.

"Now that the shock has worn off, how do you feel?" he asked Reine.

"Shaky," she admitted. "But intact. All body parts accounted for."

Thank God. And yet he couldn't miss the quiver in her voice.

"I was wondering why Bixler's bodyguards disappeared," he said. "Now we know."

"Not hardly. At least not the driver of the Monte Carlo. I got up close and personal with him, even if it was only for a split second."

"You can identify him?"

"I'll never forget that snarl," she said. "This morning, the guy with the fair hair talking to Ozzie Skinner—he had this weird little scar that tugged at the side of his lip. That's what I saw in that instant I was up against the windshield."

"You're sure?"

"Positive. As for those particular low riders—both of them were parked at the truck stop this morning."

"Then Bixler might not be responsible, after all."

"This guy could still work for him," Reine reasoned. "He could have gotten to Skinner, maybe paid him to be his eyes and ears around the spread.

It's not like Skinner's a loyal employee. He's a drifter.''

''You're right. And snarl-boy's being with Skinner just this morning, then showing up here, is carrying coincidence a little too far.''

The various possibilities ran through Cash's mind for the rest of the drive.

The house was dark as he pulled the car into the compound. Which wasn't surprising. His mother tended to go to bed early and rise with the sun. Besides, her rooms were in the rear quadrant of the hacienda.

Cash took the gun with him when he climbed out of the driver's seat. He stuck the weapon into the back of his waistband. By the time he rounded the car, Reine had already opened the passenger door.

The full moon allowed him to see the tension still gripping her. He took care of the door and placed a hand on the side of her waist as they walked to the house. When he felt her shudder, he swung her into his arms.

At the same time a breeze picked up and swept across the walkway, rocking the swing, which filled the quiet night with unexpected sound.

''I love how it creaks,'' she murmured against his chest.

''Yeah. Me, too.''

Feeling things he couldn't even name, Cash held Reine close and stroked the back of her head.

''When I first saw it,'' she said softly, ''I almost thought it was the one from the ranch.''

''You really imagined the old man would let me have a single thing that was his?''

''I'm sorry,'' she murmured, slipping her hands up

his chest and around his neck. "I'm so sorry about what he did to you." She tilted her head and met his gaze. "I never had a chance to tell you that before."

"Because I didn't let you. And I'm sorry about that."

"You ought to be," Reine said, giving him a half-hearted shove.

Not that he let her go.

His arms still around her, Cash said, "When I saw the swing at some flea market, all I could think about was you and me on it...talking...holding hands... kissing...."

He stared deep into her eyes, wanting in the worst way to kiss her now.

"Is that why you bought it?"

Rather than answering her with words, he danced her to the swing, twirled her around and fell back, taking her with him. They were both laughing as she landed on top of him. The swing bounced—and creaked—in earnest.

Cash was instantly catapulted back in time to a day he'd never forget—the day he'd realized he didn't just love Reine; he was *in love* with her. They'd been huddled together on that old swing, sharing dreams for the future. He'd thought then that no one and nothing could ever come between them.

But something had, and only a few months later.

For years, he'd blamed the old man for being the cause, but Cash had to admit that wasn't fair. Losing Reine had been his own fault. He himself had gotten between them.

He pulled her closer and laced his fingers through her hair, felt her forehead nest against his cheek and her breath whisper over his throat.

He wanted another chance. Wanted to do it right this time.

"I want you, Reine," he murmured.

She raised her head to look at him. "So you say."

She was so beautiful in the moonlight—or in the sunlight, or in the dark. He didn't have to see her to experience her beauty. It was something she carried inside her, something that shone out of her with every smile—no—with every beat of her heart.

He cupped her cheek, loving its softness. *Loving her.*

Reine dipped her head and their mouths met. Lightly. Tenderly. Then with increasing tension.

She'd never asked for much, Cash remembered. Not anything tangible, really. She'd always seemed content with exactly what she'd had. He'd put it down to her not being hungry—not for material things, that was—because of her trust fund. But he no longer thought that. Now he understood that she was content inside, with who she was, in a way that he had never been—at least, not since he'd learned the truth.

Being content with herself had always been enough for her—with the exception of other people, of course.

She'd needed love from the moment she'd arrived at Matlock Ranch. Ten years old and she'd lost both her parents. He'd pitied her, at first. But he was already loving her by the time she'd admitted that her biggest fear was of being abandoned again by the people she most cared about.

And that was exactly what he'd done.

"Reine, I really *am* sorry," he murmured, kissing

every inch of her face before settling on her lips once more.

If anything had happened to her, he would have blamed himself for that, too.

Nothing bad could ever happen to her. He'd see to it, Cash promised himself, feeling like a man suddenly obsessed.

He wanted her. Wanted to make her his.

Physically…

Emotionally…

In every way possible.

Deepening the kiss, he felt her response, not just in her lips or in the tongue that boldly sought his, but in the subtle movements of her body. The way she settled over him. Molded herself to him.

He knew they would still be a perfect fit.

Cupping her buttocks, he pushed up so she could feel him, hard and heavy with desire for her.

Reine moaned into his mouth and the sound sent him deeper to a place he couldn't leave.

Didn't want to leave.

Determined to bring her there instead, Cash tugged at her skirts, exposing her to the night. Her flesh was warm, supple, sensitive. She shuddered at his touch.

Then she edged to the side and he felt her hand at his waist. He sucked in his breath when she found his belt buckle and released it. His zipper came next. And then she burrowed beneath the layers of clothing and found him.

He filled her hand the way he wanted to fill her inside.

Unable to think of anything else, he slipped his fingers beneath the elastic of her panties and around to the front of her where he found her hot and wet and hungry for him.

He shifted, pushed the panties to the side so sharply that he heard a slight sound as they tore. Then he freed himself, found her and plunged straight inside her tight, moist warmth.

She cried out, and he feared that he'd hurt her.

She was too tight, as if it had been a long time since she'd had a lover. A *very* long time. And yet, within seconds, she pushed herself up from his chest and sank down on his entire length. Her fingers dug into his shoulders.

Neither of them moved for a moment.

"I've dreamed of this," she murmured, her breathing seductively heavy.

Though hooded, her eyes were open, devouring his face the way she was devouring him inside her.

He anchored her hips and thrust higher.

Reine cried out again, and the sound was echoed by the creak of the swing as it followed their subtle motions. As they rocked together, she threw back her head, arched her spine and slowly raised her arms.

She hooked her hands under her hair and lifted it, as though she was trying to find a breeze to cool the back of her neck. The graceful movement lifted the fullness of her breasts, as well, and Cash was mesmerized by the sight. Then she sighed, releasing her hair, and trailed her fingers along her throat, over the material covering her breasts and belly to the place where they were intimately joined.

She never stopped watching his face as she slid her hands, slowly upward again and under her top, to where they lingered on her breasts.

Watching Reine touch herself drove Cash beyond

patience. Waiting no longer, he began to move inside her, satisfied when she matched his rhythm. Then she slipped her hands down her belly so she could touch him. He hooked an arm around her waist and tugged until she lay forward, where he could taste the breasts to which she'd so seductively brought his attention.

He suckled her nipples through the soft fabric, urging her to new heights of passion.

Then he reached under her top and fingered her through the fine lace of her bra, reveling in the tensing of her nipples into buds. A cry caught in her throat, and he swiftly plunged one hand down to find yet a third bud—her erotic center.

He'd barely touched her when he felt her tighten around him. She pulsed, the strokes intense along his length all the way to his tip. Suddenly he was lost, shuddering against her, dying the little death, welcoming it not only for him, but especially for her....

Only afterward, cradling Reine while they were still joined, feeling the cold steel of his handgun pressed into his back, did Cash recognize the irony of that wish.

"JASPER, WE NEED TO TALK about Gray."

Marlene entered his office. His sanctuary. The place he came to pray that his son would truly remain unharmed. Jasper stared at his wife through bloodshot eyes and regretted not being able to share his grief with her.

He was sober now and wondering what terrible things he might have said to hurt her this time.

"I know how upset you are, Marlene. So am I."

Jasper rose from his desk chair and went to her. As usual, he didn't know how to be of comfort. He stood over her, his arms dangling at his sides but aching to hold her.

"I'm gonna make Cash pay for your grief," he promised.

Marlene stiffened and moved away from him. "Cash had nothing to do with Gray's kidnapping!" she insisted. "He's been trying to help."

"That's what he wants you to think, but—"

"Stop it! I've had enough of your paranoia and anger and guilt. This is our son's life we're talking about. If we don't give over the money…"

A part of him feared that she was right—a part that he couldn't afford to listen to. He believed what he had to so that he wouldn't go out of his mind.

"I told you we don't have the money."

"Then we'll get it."

"Matlock Construction is tapped out." He shouldn't have tried to hide this trouble from her for so long. Now she just didn't understand. "The company's nearly worthless."

"But we still have the ranch. The property along the river hasn't lost its value."

"I told you before, I'm not selling!"

She hesitated for only a second before saying, "Then *I* will."

"Not without my signature."

"Don't make me force the issue, Jasper."

He stared. She was so calm and self-assured. He hadn't seen her like this since Gray had been snatched. Her determined expression triggered his fear.

"Don't you threaten *me*, woman. What makes you think you can bend me to your will?"

What did she know?

When she said, "Divorce…I'll divorce you if I must," he was certain she'd found out about Selena Cullen.

His one foolish misstep in the thirty-five years of their marriage now threatened to end it. He'd been digging around about Jimmy Cullen's company when he'd met Selena. She'd come on to him. Later, he'd realized she'd figured he could do something to help her kid.

So he guessed they'd used each other.

He had no excuse except that he'd been desperate over the possibility of losing Matlock Construction at the time. And he'd been too damn weak. Marlene had been giving him flak about him and Cash. His ego had been sorely in need of bolstering and Selena had been so willing to assuage it.

Surely one slip was not enough reason to end a solid marriage that had spanned more than three decades.…

"Where will getting rid of me get you?" he asked, trying to keep calm.

"If we divorce, you lose your stake in the property I brought with me when we married."

Jasper couldn't help himself. He laughed. "Hell if I do."

"Papa told me so," Marlene said with confidence. "He had the lawyers set it up and assured me you'd agreed to it!"

"We had an agreement, all right. If *I* leave *you,* then I have no claim on that river property. It reverts to you and any children we have. But I'm going nowhere, Marlene. And neither is that land."

His gut twisted inside when the realization hit her

like a ton of adobe bricks. Her expression crumpled and tears burst from her eyes in a sudden torrent.

But the thing that really got to him, was her terrified "Oh, no...Gray!"

The wail screeched straight up his spine, piercing his poor excuse of a heart.

HE'D ALMOST MANAGED IT. Even as he thought he couldn't stand the tension gripping his shoulders and back a moment longer, Gray could feel the rope start to give.

He repositioned his wrists slightly and rubbed the tether harder against the sharp edge of the stone. A few more strokes and his hands suddenly sprang free of each other.

Sucking in a shaky breath, he brought his arms in front of him. They'd been pulled back, his hands tied together, for so much of the past days that he could hardly feel them, let alone move them properly. He'd been untied whenever they came to feed him and let him relieve himself outside—at gunpoint, of course—and each time, getting himself moving had been harder than the last.

His blood was flowing freely now, and sensation started returning in waves of pain.

He ripped the tape from across his mouth and nearly yowled when it seemed to take a layer of his skin and beard stubble with it.

"Pain's good," he muttered, keeping the sensation in perspective. "Tells you that you're alive."

Alive and free at last!

Well...almost. He still had to deal with the ropes around his ankles.

If only his fingers would work right. Awkward,

only half alive, they fumbled with the knots, couldn't even loosen them. It was like trying to get an old shoe off a horse's hoof with his bare hands.

Gray swore. Though he had no way of knowing the exact time, he'd bet the first streaks of sunrise wouldn't be long in coming. If experience served him, one of his captors would be back to check on him any time now....

He flexed his fingers to pump blood to their tips and tried again.

Feeling the first knot loosen, he kept working at it until it came undone. Then the next. And the last.

Finally, the rope fell away.

He rotated his ankles and tried to determine if he could still feel all his toes.

It doesn't matter. Just stand up, dammit!

Which he did. With difficulty. He was so stiff and sore, he felt as if he'd been pummeled.

At least his brain wasn't too drugged—not like before. He'd feigned indifference to the food the last time they'd been there, had acted groggy and kind of sick and had barely eaten enough to satisfy them.

Gray eased himself to the doorway. Each step brought more life to his limbs. He fought past the pain and got himself outside into the dark.

But no sooner did he take his first breath of freedom than he heard the soft snort of a horse echo from upstream.

He bolted into the brush.

There was nowhere for him to go, this being a box canyon and all. What the hell was he going to do?

Though he was able to navigate, trying to fight his way out before all his faculties returned would be suicide. The bastard would stop him dead.

He had to make a run for it.

Using boulders and bushes as cover, he worked his way toward the mouth of the canyon, directly toward the soft clop-clop of the horse threading its way alongside the stream. He moved steadily if furtively, pausing only when mount and rider came so close he could reach out and touch them.

His eyes accustomed to the dark from living in it, Gray could see the man's rifle and wondered what the odds were that he could get his hands on the weapon if he surprised the bastard and pummeled him into the ground.

Not good. Not yet.

Therefore he remained still and fought the urge, letting horse and rider pass.

Pumped with adrenaline, he started off again, keeping his ears sharply attuned to the movement behind him, knowing exactly when the horse stopped and the rider dismounted.

Gray figured he had only a few minutes before his kidnapper would be on his trail—one for him to get inside, another to realize what had happened and get himself all pissed off, a third to get back outside and onto his mount.

His body finally cooperating more fully, Gray left the brush and ran alongside the stream, straight toward the mouth of the canyon. A furious ''Matlock!'' echoing after him spurred him on faster.

He ran recklessly now, knowing that, once he was outside the canyon's grip, it would be easier to get away. There were too many directions for one man to cover.

And lots of places to hide.

He knew every one of them from his childhood.

He and Cash had loved playing hide-and-seek in these hills, and eventually Reine had joined them in the game.

Gray was nearly clear of the canyon when he felt more than heard the furious pounding of hooves on stone. His kidnapper didn't seem to be looking for him at all. Maybe he figured his prey was long gone. Then he'd be hightailing it to warn his partner in crime before the law was on them.

"Matlock, I know you're out there!" the bastard's declaration disavowed him of that notion.

Gray shot out of the canyon and toward the familiar series of hills on his right. There were all kinds of places where he could hole up for a while.

But timing was not on his side.

The first faint rays of dawn were lighting the landscape even as horse and rider burst from the canyon.

Behind him, Gray could hear the man gathering up his mount, slowing him, bringing him to a dead stop.

He was almost to his goal when he heard the sharp click of metal on metal as the kidnapper readied his rifle.

"Stop, Matlock!"

But Gray decided to chance it. Functioning fine now, he could hold his own. And he was almost to a place where he could force a confrontation.

It was the bullet that brought him face-to-face with reality—the bullet and the searing pain and his own blood blooming across the front of his shirt....

Chapter Eleven

Sunday

Reine floated awake. Dust motes danced through the shaft of light that swept over the bed, and she happily tried to catch them. But they were as elusive as... well, love.

She couldn't remember ever feeling so wonderful. Or so sore. Not all of her aches were the result of her run-in with the low rider, either.

Remembering the night that had followed made her grin.

Even remembering how and why she and Cash were together didn't wipe the smile from her lips. This morning she was convinced. Together, she and Cash could do anything, even rescue Gray.

All for one and one for all...

In everything but the bedroom, of course, she thought with an unladylike snort.

Getting out of bed, she nearly tripped over the shirt Cash had discarded on the floor along with the rest of his clothing. She slipped into it, and, inhaling his fragrance with a contented sigh, wandered barefoot around the room. The sound of the shower told her where she could find Cash if she could bear to be made love to yet another time.

Then again, one more time might lead to another and another—which would be fine with her if they didn't have such pressing concerns.

Yawning, she stretched and wandered into the small gallery joining his master bedroom and office. She was admiring an R. C. Gorman watercolor—a Pueblo woman who reminded her of Luna—when the phone rang. She thought to alert Cash, then decided she might as well let the answering machine do its job.

"Cash Abreu here. State your business," came the crisp message echoing from his office.

"Abreu. We need to talk. There's a foul-up in our plan."

That sounded like Sam Valdez. Reine frowned. Surely she was mistaken.

But when the man at the other end said, "Marlene had it all wrong," her stomach clutched.

What plan could the two of them have in common? she asked herself. Something involving her aunt.

"Getting out of the marriage won't do the trick, and the old bastard won't budge," Valdez said tersely. "We're gonna have to figure out some other way to get our hands on that river property," he concluded.

That left Reine stunned.

WHEN CASH LEFT THE bathroom, he immediately zeroed in on Reine. Surprisingly, she was fully dressed—he'd been certain she'd planned on showering again, since her last shower had led to more lovemaking—and she was standing in front of the mirror, trying to tame her hair.

"Leave it. I like it wild." He wrapped his arms around her waist and thought of the long night they'd shared. "I like *you* wild."

She met his gaze in the mirror. "Is that why you went after me?"

Thinking the question oddly phrased, he murmured, "I don't get it."

"Because I'd be wild. Or was it something else altogether?"

Hearing the catch in her voice, he studied her mirror image, but her expression was impassive. Still, he had this feeling—no, a certainty—that something was wrong.

"You're in a strange mood."

"You did warn me you wanted me, Cash. Many times. Only you never said why."

"Isn't that obvious?"

"No, not really."

"For one," he said, running his knuckles down the side of her face, "look at you."

"Let's do that. I'm blond, reasonably attractive—"

"Stunning," he interrupted.

This was getting a little weird. What in hell had gone on in the ten minutes he'd left her alone to shower and dress?

She continued. "I have an okay body—"

"You don't have to be so modest. You're perfect."

"Like a piece of artwork?"

"Only you live and breathe."

"But still a possession. Something you…collect, show off to the world."

Back to that again. Was that what was bothering her? That she feared he saw her as nothing more than a possession? He shoved away the twinge of guilt when he remembered that was pretty much the way he *had* thought about her at first. But everything had changed.

He had changed.

Trying to reassure Reine, Cash said, "I thought we finished this conversation the other night."

"Not to *my* satisfaction."

Wanting to kiss away her doubts, he turned her to face him. "Let me try to satisfy you, then."

Reine shrugged away from him and wrapped her arms around her middle as if she were trying to protect herself—from him.

"A woman likes to think a man wants her for more than her looks."

"Don't you think I know there's more to you than what's in that mirror? Inside, you're rich with warmth and caring and loyalty."

All were things he'd ached for without her.

"'All for one and one for all,' right?" Her smile was bittersweet. "What's inside *you,* Cash?"

"No one's perfect, but I think you already know the good things along with the bad."

"Do I? Everything?" When he didn't answer immediately, she asked, "No secrets?"

Now Reine was scaring him. "Where are you going with this?"

"You tell me."

"Tell you what?"

The rising tension between them almost made him

shout at her. He curled his hands into fists and told himself not to lose his temper. Relationships were scary. She merely needed to be reassured.

"For starters," she was saying, "what exactly do you and Sam Valdez have in common?"

His stomach dropped. "You know. How?"

"Valdez needs to learn discretion. He called when you were in the shower, and I let the answering machine pick up. It seems that Uncle Jasper's river property won't be available to the two of you, after all."

"I can explain."

"How you and Valdez schemed to get it?"

"That was before—"

"What? Me?"

"Gray," Cash said, suddenly feeling desperate. If he didn't do this right, he was going to lose her. "Before Gray disappeared."

"Interesting. Because I don't believe that Aunt Marlene had any reason to consider selling—*before*—did she?"

Cash cursed under his breath. "You can't think that I set this whole thing up."

"Why not?"

"I would never hurt Gray any more than I would hurt you."

"Well, then, there it is," Reine said, laughing without humor. "What you did to me seventeen years ago wasn't supposed to hurt, right?" She shook her head. "It would be ironic if Uncle Jasper had you pinned all along."

"I swear to you that I had nothing to do with Gray's kidnapping."

"Just as you had nothing to do with trying to destroy Matlock Construction?"

"It's not the same thing."

"No? You vowed to strip Uncle Jasper of everything he ever cared about. He does care about both his son and his company, if not with equal fervor. And though he gives me a hard time, he cares for me, too. He would hate knowing I'd succumbed to your charms again. The only things left out of the equation are Matlock Ranch and his marriage to my aunt, both of which could have gone down with one genius stroke. Well, almost genius. You still have some work to do there."

Cash knew that, everything combined, she had reason to be upset. It looked bad. And yet he couldn't help being angry. Did she think so little of him? Did she not believe a word that came out of his mouth?

"I didn't use Marlene any more than I'm using you," he said. "She went to Valdez with the offer. And I never agreed to it. You've got it all wrong, Reine."

"What about Sam Valdez? Did he have it wrong when he said 'our plan'?"

"I told him I'd have to think about the offer and I have. I decided I couldn't do it. I couldn't steal my own brother's 'legacy,' as you so aptly called it. And I couldn't betray *you* that way."

"Then why didn't you tell me about it?"

"*This* is why. Your attitude. Your assumptions. You don't trust me."

"And why should I?"

"Because, whatever else I've done, I've never lied to you, Reine."

"Never? You once told me you loved me. And the next day you were gone."

Cash was furious. His loving her hadn't been a lie. Circumstances—namely, Jasper Matlock—had driven him from her. And he'd been a plain fool to let it happen.

Why couldn't she see that?

Either she believed in him or she didn't, and he feared he knew which direction the wind was blowing.

"I'm through with this," he said coldly.

Her expression stricken, she whispered, "Then so am I."

When she rushed out of the room, he didn't try to stop her. Instead, he picked up the nearest thing at hand—a century-old ceramic bowl he'd paid a fortune for at auction—and threw it against the wall. Its shattering into pieces didn't make him feel any better.

He stood there, staring at them, stunned.

What the hell had just happened?

It couldn't be over. Not this time.

And where did Reine think she was going without a car?

Cash stormed through the house, expecting Reine to be cooling her heels in the drive.

She wasn't there.

Standing next to the swing where they'd made love the night before, he watched her cut across his land on foot, knowing exactly where she was headed.

He would have expected her to be angry and disappointed at learning he'd been plotting with Valdez, but her reaction had been out of hand. Why was she so ready to believe the worst of him at every turn?

Ready to believe Jasper Matlock over him.

Ready to stand by Matlock's side rather than his! *Again*.

History was repeating itself and Cash feared that no matter what he did, he couldn't alter it.

BY THE TIME SHE CAME within sight of the house, having walked for a couple of hours, Reine was exhausted physically as well as emotionally.

With every step she'd taken across the rocky land, she'd gone over and over the argument until she was sick to death of it. Considering the circumstances, she just couldn't see how things could have turned out any differently.

Whether or not she believed Cash was responsible for Gray's disappearance—which she didn't, really—was *not* the issue. She'd let him think as much just to hurt him the way she'd been hurting. That he had been plotting with Valdez to get the land for who knew how long had only a perfunctory bearing on the way she felt.

That Cash had known about Aunt Marlene, however, had been an involved party to the proposition, and that he hadn't told her even when he'd decided to pass on the deal—those had been the deciding factors in her mind.

Which wasn't to dismiss her very real fears of Cash wanting her in the same way as he did any of his possessions. Except she had added value, Reine reminded herself, still suspecting that part of the allure of having her was knowing what that would do to Uncle Jasper.

And Cash had let her walk out the door so easily....

That *she* had known about Marlene's going to Valdez, and hadn't told Cash didn't enter into the picture, Reine had decided. It had been her aunt's confidence to share, and her responsibility to keep her mouth shut. She'd had nothing to gain from the situation.

With that justification firmly fixed in her mind, Reine entered the house and practically ran into her uncle, who seemed to be in a hurry to leave.

"Have you heard anything?" she asked anxiously.

He shook his head. "Not yet. Where have you been? I expected you to make a pest of yourself and I've hardly seen you around."

"I've been busy."

He stared at her and scowled as if he could read her mind. To her surprise, he didn't comment, but said, "I've got some business to take care of."

"On Sunday?" she asked.

"This can't wait." Jasper started to pass her, then hesitated. He reached out and gently pushed a strand of her hair away from her forehead. "You always did look pretty when you let your hair down."

Then he left and Reine had trouble swallowing past the lump in her throat. Uncle Jasper paid so few compliments, his words were akin to his telling her he loved her.

Before going upstairs, she decided to check the dayroom for her aunt. Marlene was asleep on the chaise longue, her swollen and tearstained face at peace for the moment. Crying inside, herself, she wanted nothing more than to feel her aunt's arms around her and to hear a few words of comfort. But, certain that Marlene had none to give, and fearing that heaping anything more on the poor woman would be too much for her to bear, Reine decided to let her be.

She went upstairs, to the rooms that were still hers. Several changes of clothing hung in her closet. Considering how much time she spent at the ranch, it had seemed foolish dragging things back and forth. She had everything she needed here.

Everything but Cash.

Heartbroken, she stepped into the shower, determined to wash away the lingering scent of him. She scrubbed and scrubbed her skin, but still she could smell him…taste him…feel him. Finally, hot water beating down on her, she gave in to tears. A good cry should make her feel better.

Only it didn't.

Nothing would ever make her feel better again— except maybe doing something more about Gray.

So, washed and dressed in jeans and a cotton shirt, Reine left the house and borrowed the old four-by-four Uncle Jasper kept threatening to consign to the junk heap.

Tobiah Hill had a small place of his own on the property just up the road; the same house that had been assigned to Zane Abreu when he'd been foreman.

How many times had she played with Cash and Gray in its front yard? How many times had Luna fed them all in her tiny kitchen?

Reine tried not to let childhood memories intrude when she parked and left the vehicle.

Apparently having heard her drive up, Tobiah looked out at her from the front-room window. She waved at him. A moment later, he met her on the porch.

"Something wrong at the house?" he immediately asked, his brow wrinkled in concern.

"Yes. Gray still isn't home. That's why I'm here."

"Don't know anything more'n I did yesterday," he warned her.

"Maybe yesterday I didn't think of all the right questions to ask."

"Want to come in?"

Wanting to keep the emotional memories to a minimum, Reine indicated the weathered wooden chairs facing each other on the porch. "Out here'll do. This won't take long."

"Fine by me."

Tobiah waited until she was seated before settling in the other chair.

"How well do you know Ozzie Skinner?" she asked.

"Skinner? He's a drifter. Comes and goes. At the moment, he's gone."

"You did fire him, then."

"Nope. Didn't have to. He collected his week's pay and told me to expect him when I saw him."

Which made the man sound like he could be the kidnapper, Reine thought. Or one of them. He'd had easy access to both the ranch and Gray.

"I told him not to bother coming back," Tobiah added. "What's your interest?"

"Yesterday morning Skinner was in Española when I figured he should have been working."

"He reported on time—must've sneaked away. Can't say as I'm surprised. Wasn't the first time no one could find him during the last week or so."

Because he'd been sneaking around, plotting? Then checking in with a cohort?

"I saw him with a fair-haired man," Reine went on, "who had a scar here." She indicated the spot on her own lip. "Made him look like he was snarling. Then last night, when Cash and I were trying to find out what happened to Gray, someone tried running me over in a low rider. I got a glimpse of the driver—Skinner's friend."

"Closer'n that," Tobiah said. "That'd be his cousin, Lloyd Rynko. He's a bad one. Spent some time in the pen."

Reine's pulse quickened. "For what?"

"Grand theft auto…and for murder."

JASPER COULDN'T BELIEVE he'd come to this, crawling to a man like Evan Bixler for help. From the other side of the bar, the smug son of a bitch was smiling at him through a thick wreath of cigar smoke.

"Well, Matlock, never thought I'd see you step foot in my establishment."

Jasper sat himself at the bar. "Never thought I'd be in some place called The Bix Box, neither."

"The first drink's on the house. What can I get you?"

"I'm not here to drink."

"Then, what can I do for you?"

Though he was sweating inside, Jasper tried to remain cool. He was hoping to add a couple of hundred thousand to what he could scrape together from his and Marlene's personal worth. Then he'd see what he could work out about the river property—maybe remortgage it. He was willing to grasp any straw offered. Gray's life might depend on it.

He was done with fooling himself.

"It's what I can do for you," he told Bixler with a hearty smile. "I gave your offer on Matlock Construction due consideration."

"I recollect your turning me down flat."

"Then I decided I was too hasty and thought again. I'm ready to sell."

"How interesting. And how fortuitous for you— your son is ready to buy."

"Gray?" Jasper popped off his stool and leaned across the bar to grab Bixler's shirtfront. "*You* know where my boy is, you'd better tell me!"

"Whoa! I'm talking about Cash Abreu."

Instantly deflated, Jasper let go of Bixler's shirt and sank back to his seat, only then noticing the two hulks who'd moved in on him. Bodyguard types. Bixler gave them the high sign and they backed off.

Jasper ran his hand through his hair. "Cash tell you he's my son?"

"I do my homework."

"But what's he got to do with you?"

"He suggested we become partners in taking over Matlock Construction."

"Bastard!"

"He *is* that, isn't he?" Bixler agreed. "But he is willing to buy, while I... Well, I've lost interest—in Matlock Construction, anyway."

"What else is there?"

Bixler was relighting his cigar. He puffed and puffed, making Jasper wait until his skin crawled.

Finally, the other man said, "Let's you and me talk about Matlock Ranch."

TAKING A DEEP BREATH, Marlene rehearsed what she was going to say, but all the words flew from her mind when the door opened and she found herself facing Luna Abreu, who'd been her friend once, long ago.

"Marlene, come in. Any word on your son?"

She shook her head. "I'm afraid not."

"I'm so sorry," Luna told her, taking her hand. "I've always had a spot for Gray in my heart."

Marlene's eyes stung. "I know he feels the same for you."

"You want to see Cash."

"Please."

"Come with me."

The walk through Cash's house was one of the longest Marlene had ever taken. The rooms blurred together. Suddenly she was in his office. Cash was on the phone, and it sounded as if he was closing some kind of big money deal.

"Tomorrow, then," he finally said, hanging up the phone. "Marlene." If he was surprised to see her, he didn't show it. "Any news?"

She shook her head and wrapped her arms around her middle.

"I'll leave you alone," Luna said and turned away.

Cash rose and indicated a small couch near the fireplace. "Please, sit."

"No. I'm fine." Before she lost her nerve, Marlene said, "I'm here to sell you my half of the river property."

"Marlene—"

"Please. For Gray. Jasper won't budge on this, Cash. He won't let go. He cares more for that cursed

land than our son. I don't know how else to save
him.''

"I can't do it, Marlene.''

"Can't? Or won't?''

"Won't, then—''

"Oh, my God, what am I going to do?'' she
wailed, all hope lost.

She'd made Sam the same offer, but he'd told her
he couldn't get his hands on the money for a few
days. A few days would be too late.

"Listen, take it easy—''

"'Easy'? Gray is your brother!''

"That's why I can't buy the land from you. It's
his heritage, and it would be like my stealing from
him.''

"What does it matter who owns the land if my
son is dead!''

"You don't understand.''

"You're right, I don't!'' Marlene cried, backing
away from him. "I don't understand why I'm going
to lose my only child.''

With that she scurried out of the room.

"Marlene, you're not going to lose him!'' Chase
called after her. "Not if I can help it.''

But she closed her ears to that lie and to any others
he might try to tell her.

Chapter Twelve

Some idiocy prompted Reine to swing by the old chile mill on her way home, near sundown. The four-by-four was sturdy enough to get over any terrain, though her back was another story. The shocks on the old vehicle were history. She only drove to the mouth of the canyon before getting out and walking.

The long shadows that preceded nightfall filled the space, making it appear as depressed as she felt.

She'd failed Gray.

Cash had failed her.

Or rather, he had betrayed her. Betrayed *them.*

All for one and one for all...

Had the oath always been a lie?

With each step, memories cascaded over her until she was surrounded by the past. Every rock, every tree, every scurry of some unseen animal reminded her of Cash.

This had been their childhood playground.

The site of their initiation into adulthood.

Once, this had been the most significant place in her heart. Now, the sight of the abandoned mill nearly did her in.

Her pulse jagging wildly, she decided to go inside

anyway. Perhaps by revisiting the haunt where she'd lost her virginity to Cash—not to mention where Uncle Jasper had caught them together and had nearly killed Cash in his fury—she would be able to expurgate him from her soul.

But the very act of entering the building sent her emotions reeling. Every inch of the familiar space made her think about him. About her own foolishness in opening herself up to him again. About his being the only man she'd ever loved.

She'd never stopped—not once through all those lonely years.

She'd never even given another man a fair chance.

Rather, she'd vested herself in work that was satisfying, and in the little family she had.

Now everything had changed.

Aunt Marlene and Uncle Jasper—her surrogate parents—were at odds with each other, might even divorce. Gray—closer than a first cousin, more like a brother—was gone, maybe for good. To get him back safely, the ranch would have to be divided, even as were the hearts of its owners.

She feared nothing would ever be the same again.

Everything really had changed, Reine thought with a lump in her throat; all but her work—and that would still be waiting for her. When this was over, she would throw herself into it completely. She would lose herself in helping other people's children rather than the ones she didn't have. Would probably never have.

Most important, she would try to forget that Cash Abreu ever existed.

Blindly staring into the room, she suddenly focused on what looked like some refuse in one corner.

Frowning, she drew closer until she could make out a bedroll laid out as if it had been recently used.

And, unless she was crazy, she smelled the lingering odor of food. Tamales? And something far less tempting—stale cigar smoke.

Someone had been using the old mill for shelter and might be returning at any time.

Uneasy, not up to a confrontation of any sort, Reine had barely decided to leave when she noticed something else that was strange. Frowning, she crossed the few yards to the bedroll and stooped down to retrieve a piece of rope two yards or so in length. Odd. Then she saw another piece.

Reaching for it, she had the weirdest feeling. Indeed, she discovered the rope had been split in two—*shredded* in two. And on the floor next to the bedroll, lay a rock.

She ran a finger along its sharp edge....

Suddenly, she realized she'd stopped breathing and gasped for air.

Her imagination was running wild.

Could it be?

Rising on shaky legs, Reine peered around into every dark corner. She blinked as if she were seeing things when her gaze lit on another discarded object.

A man's hat.

She stood and stared for a moment, before moving to pick it up. Her hands shook as she turned it to inspect the band. Even before her gaze lit on the small pin—a silver feather—she knew the hat was Gray's!

Touching something that belonged to her cousin was almost as good as touching the man himself. Her mind worked furiously as she considered the possibilities. Suddenly, a weight lifted from her soul.

He'd been here—*right here*—all along!

And from the looks of it, he'd escaped. And from the smell of it, fairly recently.

Then where was he?

Why hadn't he gone straight for the house?

His hat in her hands, she ran from the building, screaming, "Gray!" Her voice bounced throughout the canyon, coming back in a hollow echo to mock her.

Of course he was on his way home. Maybe he'd arrived there while she'd been talking to Tobiah.

Her step far lighter than it had been on the way in, Reine retreated, but still she continued scouring the dimly lit canyon for any further signs of her cousin. Cash had taught her how to track long ago. She spotted prints made by horses along the streambed, from when she and Cash had ridden in, no doubt. But nothing made by a human.

Still, she continued to keep her eyes open and, halfway to the four-by-four, spotted some brush that had been crushed as if a person had run through it from the hillside to the trail. She checked the ground more closely: rocks spewed in every direction, an indentation caused by a boot heel.

Her breath catching in her throat, she moved faster, unable to match the much longer stride she imagined she followed—a stride made by someone tall.

Gray?

Then boot prints were obliterated by a horse's hooves churning up the ground. Someone chasing him?

Her imagination taking off now, her heart began

to thump as she passed her vehicle and saw where the horse had seemed to stop before wandering off to the hills on her right.

Surely Gray had gotten away.

She prayed to God that he would be waiting for her at the house.

But her vigilance was nearly her undoing, for she refused to go back until she could follow the tracks no longer. As the last dim light faded, she came to a place where it looked as if someone had fallen.

It was already too dark for anything but her imagination, and Reine refused to give her immediate suspicion credence.

Gray was all right, she told herself. He had to be.

She nearly flew back to the four-by-four, thinking to head for the house and driving breakneck foolish. When a particularly large rut slammed her teeth together so hard she thought her jaw went out of joint, she got hold of herself, slowed down and made toward a road that was the long route home, but would be infinitely easier on the vehicle and on her.

The longer drive gave her extra time to think.

Did she really want to raise her aunt's and uncle's expectations and at the same time worry them to death if she explained it all? For all she knew, either one of them might be reckless enough or desperate enough to go out now and try to find Gray, which surely would lead to disaster.

She couldn't say a word—not to them.

Then what should she do?

She couldn't wait around indefinitely in the hope that Gray would show. Waiting while doing nothing would make her crazy. And she couldn't keep this to herself, either. Only one course was left to her, Reine knew, if she didn't find her cousin at the house when she arrived.

And like it or not, she was going to take it.

CASH WAS STRETCHED OUT on the swing when he heard the vehicle approaching in the dark. He sat up and, in amazement, watched Reine get out of a rusty old four-by-four and stalk toward him, hat in hand. He would have bet it'd be a cold day in hell before she'd ever set foot on his place again.

She did tend to surprise him at every turn.

He was on his feet when she reached him and shoved the hat at his stomach without so much as a word.

"Thanks," he said wryly, "but I already have a few dozen of these."

"Bet you don't!" she said defiantly. "That one's Gray's. The very one he was wearing when he disappeared!"

Hope seared Cash as he grasped the felt brim tighter. "Come inside."

Reine hesitated for only a moment, then stormed into the house ahead of him. She went straight for the living room and threw herself into a safe chair rather than one of the couches where he might get too close.

The hat still in his hands, Cash chose to remain standing. "So tell me everything, from the beginning."

"I went back to the chile mill—"

"Why?"

"I just did, all right?" Sounding thoroughly defensive, she frowned at him. "Don't make a federal case of it. If you keep interrupting me, I'll never get to the point.''

''Fine,'' he agreed, figuring there was another story there—one she would refuse to relate even if pressed. ''Go on.''

''This time I went inside and found that someone else had come and gone before me.''

''You mean Gray?''

She nodded. ''The kidnapper was keeping him there.''

''Define 'keeping.'''

''As in being left tied up on a bedroll. It looked like he used a rock to saw through the ropes.''

''If he got away, then where is he?''

''Not at the house.'' Her frustration was evident in the terse reply. ''I don't have a clue.''

Cash thought about it. ''Hiding out?'' Which meant the kidnapper was or had been hot on his trail.

''I followed Gray's tracks until it got too dark to see anything or go any farther.''

''*You* tracked him?''

''Why so surprised? You taught me.''

''But after all these years?'' Considering the proper city lady she'd become… ''Who would have guessed?''

''Memories don't die just because some time passes.''

And Cash knew Reine didn't mean the tracking.

''Back at you,'' he said softly, regretting that he hadn't gone after her earlier.

''So what are we going to do?'' she asked.

Wanting in the worst way to pull Reine to her feet and kiss her breathless so she had nothing left in her with which to protest—to deny him—Cash stood firm and gripped Gray's hat with both hands.

"That depends on whether or not you're willing to give me a clean slate."

He always went after whatever he wanted with a no-holds-barred kind of attitude. But she'd drawn a line in the sand and he'd let her.

Not that he would accept that indefinitely. He didn't care what it took to get her back. He'd figure out the right thing and do it.

He loved her that much.

"I meant about Gray."

He saw that she did and decided they could wait a while longer.

"What about Gray?" asked a voice from the doorway.

Surprised, Cash whipped around. "Mom, I didn't know you were home."

"I just came in. You were so engaged, I guess you didn't hear me. Now, about Gray...?"

"Reine found the place where the kidnapper was keeping him hostage. He got away."

"But we don't know where to," Reine piped in, pushing herself up from the chair. "He didn't go back to the house, because I checked."

"He's got to be hiding out somewhere." In his mind's eye, Cash visualized the territory that once had been as familiar to him as breathing. "But why?"

"Obviously, he knows someone is on his trail," Reine said, sounding reluctant.

It was the same conclusion he'd drawn.

"Or maybe he's hurt," his mother said, sounding

deeply worried, "and can't make it back to the house."

That was something Cash didn't want to consider, not when they'd just gotten their first real break. Or rather, Reine had.

"So where has Gray been all this time?" Luna asked.

"The abandoned mill."

Her dark eyes widened. "On Matlock land. Pretty bold."

Bold, indeed, Cash thought. And yet, who would have thought he'd been right under their noses all this time. Then it hit him.

"My God, we were there," he said, stunned by the fact. "We were at the mill Friday. We didn't look for him there…didn't think…."

"Don't," Reine said. "I've already covered that territory. No way could we have guessed."

"I wonder if he knew."

His mother asked Reine, "How long ago did you say you discovered where he'd been held?"

"Only an hour or so."

Her expression changing subtly, Luna just nodded.

"I suppose you couldn't tell how long he'd been gone," Cash queried.

"Not really. But I don't think it was all that long, not with the smells and all."

"What kind of smells?"

"Food, mostly. Tamales, I think."

"Oh, dear," Luna said suddenly. "I'm getting so forgetful these days." She headed for the door. "I need to take care of something."

"Now?"

Her smile looked a bit forced to Cash when she said, "I won't be long."

With no further explanation, his mother headed out of the house. Cash just stared after her. Before he could dwell on how oddly she'd been acting lately, Reine came up behind him.

"So what are we going to do about Gray?"

"Pick up his trail and find him, I hope."

"Now?"

"I figure daybreak will do."

Although he had something else in mind—something he wanted to do *before* then—he wasn't about to tell her. She'd insist on coming, and he didn't need to worry about her back in addition to his own.

AT ABOUT MIDNIGHT, Cash left Akando in a sheltered blind with a warning to keep silent. The horse had thrown up his big head, as if he'd understood. Though Cash was already wearing a sidearm, he took with him a rifle for good measure, and a mag light clipped to his gun belt. He believed in being prepared.

To that end, he moved silently through the brush that limned the canyon's hillside, all the while keeping his eyes and ears open to any movement, any sound. But there was nothing except the gusting wind to spook him or the horse.

A weather front was moving in—of thick gray clouds overhead chased the moon. He sniffed the air, heavy with the moisture of coming rain. The prediction had been for an early morning shower, but he knew a drenching would come sooner.

A coyote howled its displeasure. No doubt he didn't want to get wet, either.

The mill came into view. Cash stopped and waited, patiently, expectantly. He wouldn't put it past the bastard who'd kidnapped Gray to return for some forgotten item.

There was no sign of life.

For the moment, at least, he knew he was alone.

Not that he'd had to be, but he hadn't been willing to put Reine in potential jeopardy, just in case. The low rider incident was indelibly etched in his memory.

Knowing that nothing would stop her once the sun rose, he'd agreed to meet Reine here at first light. Until then, he was going to have himself a good look around, make certain the area was safe and secure it for her arrival.

Entering the abandoned building, he snapped on the mag light.

The bedroll and ropes were as Reine had described them. But there was so much more—little details she'd neglected to mention or hadn't noticed.

A small bag lay in one corner. He opened it and the food smell she'd described assaulted him—some dried sauce on the paper. A couple of crushed beer cans formed a little pile near the wall, as if someone had been sitting there, watching over Gray as he slept.

Or had they talked?

Surely not, or Gray would be able to point a finger at his kidnapper. Not a safe situation at all.

Spotting something small and shiny near his boot toe, he bent over to pick up the item—and recognized it as a paper ring from a cigar.

The kind Evan Bixler smoked?

Cash didn't have time to wonder before he heard

the distant sound of a vehicle above the rising wind. He shut off his light at the same time the driver cut the engine.

Pulse thrumming, he slipped out of the building and silently glided a few yards up the hillside to a bent cottonwood, where he lost himself in some of its lower branches. He hunkered down and waited, the skin along his spine crawling each time wind shimmied the leaves or shook some loose board on the building.

Finally, between gusts, he heard the shuffling of boots against rocky soil. A break in the clouds revealed some movement, but the swaying of a branch before his eyes kept him from seeing more.

Then, when clouds swallowed the moon yet again, he was dependent on following the intruder by sound. He was moving closer and closer, straight for the mill.

The moment a boot hit board, Cash shouldered his rifle and snapped on his mag light, snarling, "Stop right there and turn around!"

The person below followed directions.

Cash didn't know why he was surprised when he heard Reine say, "Abreu, I knew I couldn't trust you!"

"WHAT IF IT HADN'T BEEN me in that tree?" Cash demanded, the moment he stepped close enough that they were practically nose-to-nose.

"But it was you, so it's a moot point, isn't it?"

Reine couldn't believe he was acting all macho-protective when he should be on the defensive.

Instinct had told her Cash wouldn't wait until dawn to ride out. When she hadn't been able to sleep, she'd decided to be a one-woman welcoming committee, to prevent him from acting without her. She hadn't counted on his beating her to the mill.

Feeling droplets of water splash against her face, she said, ''We'd better take shelter if we don't want to be soaked.''

Inside, the only place to sit in any comfort was the bedroll. Reine avoided it, sauntering across the floor to a gaping hole that used to hold a window. Gusts of damp air assaulted her. Needing to stay sharp around Cash, she wedged a shoulder against an exposed joint and stared out into the rainy night.

Hopefully, any traces of Gray wouldn't be washed away....

''Do you really not trust me?''

Cash's soft question came from so close it made her tremble. ''How do you expect me to answer that?'' She turned, but could barely see more than Cash's silhouette. ''Should I lie?''

''I was hoping you wouldn't have to.''

''And I was hoping you were being totally upfront with me. No, not hoping. Expecting. Believing. I guess the thought that you might have some ulterior motive for going along with me in this search just never came up in my mind.''

''My deal with Valdez had nothing to do with you.''

''Please.''

''It didn't.''

''What does it matter now, anyway?''

''What you think of me *does* matter, Reine. And you can't think too badly of me deep down, because it's me you came to for help, isn't it?''

''I do believe you don't want anything bad to happen to Gray," she admitted, steeling herself against the emotions he always stirred up in her. "That has nothing to do with us."

"It has everything to do with us."

His moving even closer both thrilled and frightened her. She didn't want to lose her head only to open her eyes to more unpleasant facts about the man.

She put out a hand. "Keep your distance."

"Afraid of your dark side, Reine?" Cash asked. "The part of you that still wants me no matter what you think I've done?"

"Get over yourself," she said without much conviction.

"I'm trying to be honest."

"Stop trying and *be* honest."

"What would you have me do, Reine?"

"For one, stop your vendetta against Uncle Jasper." She could sense his immediate withdrawal. "You've been telling yourself and anyone who'll listen that destroying Matlock Construction is just business, but that's a lie and we both know it."

"I already decided you were right about the ranch being Gray's inheritance. I won't go after it again."

That was a move in the right direction, if not exactly what she'd asked for.

"How about you?" he asked. "When will you stop choosing the old man over me?"

"Is that how you see it?"

"That's how it is. How it has been since he caught us together right here. You remember that, don't you, Reine."

She remembered every wonderful minute they'd spent together. And the terrible aftermath. She couldn't justify what Uncle Jasper had done—violence was never justified—but she thought she understood.

"Uncle Jasper is like my father, Cash. I think you held that against me…and that was the reason you shoved me out of your life, just like you did Gray. But Aunt Marlene and Uncle Jasper took care of me and loved me when I had no one else. I couldn't turn my back on him."

"And you still won't."

"Is that what you think I should do?"

His silence was his answer.

"For what it's worth," she said, "I don't think he hates you, Cash. He's obsessed with you just as you are with him."

"Ha! He wishes I'd never been born."

"I think his feelings are far more complex. Don't you think it's weird that he didn't send Luna away somewhere else to have her child? Instead, he tied her—and you—to this spread by getting Zane to marry her."

"So what do you propose he had in mind for my future? Taking over as foreman when my daddy retired?"

"Why not? Then you would have stuck around forever, had a relationship with your brother—"

"Who he forbade to hang out with me."

"I think he suddenly got scared that one of you would figure it out because you were unnaturally close for friends. I think guilt eats at him always for having made a pact with the devil—not that he'd admit it. And he may have married for the wrong reason, but he grew to love Aunt Marlene. He's loyal to her and to Gray, and what he might feel for you tears at that loyalty, so he strikes out. It's not right, but what you've been doing to him is no better. This greed of yours is a grown-up's ploy for attention. You want his and you're speaking to him in a voice he understands.''

''I vowed to strip him of what he cares about because of what he did to my mother.''

''No, that's an excuse, Cash. Luna has always wanted you to let go just as she has. But you're hurt because you think Jasper Matlock doesn't care about the natural relationship he has with you. *You care,* or you *really* would have walked away and never looked back as soon as you were able. But you couldn't do that any more than he could let you go.''

Cash had no response. Tension radiated from him but he was a master at control, even over himself.

Sighing, Reine moved from the window to the bedroll. Trying to make herself comfortable was futile. She lay there, listening to the drumming on the roof and the sound of leaks all around her.

It was going to be a long night.

Monday

A NIGHT HAD NEVER LASTED so long, but finally the sky lightened and Cash could put the thoughts that had been eating at him for hours to the back of his mind. At least for a while. He'd have to deal with them sometime. Soon, he supposed.

He wondered how so young a woman as Reine had gotten such wisdom.

Even as he pushed himself up from the spot where he'd sat all night, his back to the wall, Reine stirred on the bedroll.

"What time is it?" she asked with a big yawn.

Her golden hair was tousled around her face, and her eyes were only half open. Her lovely face was sleep-filled and sexy. He'd never get tired of seeing her like this...and he knew damn well he might never see her like this again.

"Time to find the third musketeer," he said, moving over to the bedroll and holding out his hand.

Assuming Gray was findable, he thought.

Seeming reluctant at first, Reine finally allowed him to help her to her feet. The warmth of sleep radiated from her, enticing him...

It took all his will to step back.

"Rain's stopped," she murmured in a husky voice.

"More than an hour ago."

Her concerned gaze met his. "Did you sleep at all?"

"Some."

A few minutes here and there. Not that he couldn't function no matter the circumstances, and right now he was running on pure adrenaline. There was so much to do, so little time. If they didn't find Gray now, though, he'd switch to Plan B.

Leaving the mill, Cash fetched Akando and they set out on foot. Reine showed him where she'd thought Gray had broken from the brush to the path. The prints she'd followed were half washed away, but Cash was as certain as she was that they were Gray's.

They passed the vehicle Reine had left at the mouth of the canyon. She led him off to the right. They hadn't gone uphill very far when she stopped.

"This is as far as I got last night," she said. "It looked like he might have fallen here."

A little fact that she'd omitted, Cash thought, though he didn't comment as he stooped to examine the area more closely. Although the rain had made things more difficult, it had stayed light enough that it hadn't done much damage.

That was why he was concerned when he saw a discoloration lingering along the roots of some plant life. He dipped his fingers into it. The tips came away a washed-out brown, almost like rust.

Only he knew it wasn't.

"What?" Reine asked, her voice tight when he rose without saying anything and picked up some more tracks. "Cash!"

Ignoring her plea, he tightened his grip on Akando's reins as he followed the scuffs in the earth a hundred yards or so until they disappeared as they got to the rocks. He secured the horse, then kept going, looking for some kind of hiding place. Finally he saw it—a narrow opening, barely wide enough for a man to wedge himself in. But once inside, he would be nearly invisible unless a pursuer came right up to the entrance.

Reine was directly behind him, literally breathing down his neck, as he examined the area carefully. Then he found it. More of the rust-colored stain. Only this one hadn't been washed by the rain because it had been protected. And there was so much of it, it made his stomach knot.

Cash swore and barely resisted the temptation to slam his fist into the rock.

Beside him, Reine was silent but for her ragged

breathing. He looked into her eyes. She already knew, but he had to say it anyway.

"The bastard shot him, Reine."

What he couldn't put into words was that they were back to where they'd started: not knowing if Gray was even alive.

Chapter Thirteen

"We'll have the money, Marlene," Jasper told his wife at noon when she entered his office at his request. He watched her expression lighten with hope and knew he'd done right. "We're gonna get our boy back."

"I—I don't understand. How?"

"I agreed to sell the ranch."

Evan Bixler had seemed to take particular pleasure in that agreement, as if he'd been getting what was due him. And all because Jasper had refused to let the man buy into his construction business.

"You mean you've finally agreed to let go of the river property?" Marlene asked.

"No. I'm talking about the whole damn thing. He wouldn't buy it any other way."

He didn't even know why a man like Bixler wanted rangeland. He wasn't a cowman and never would be. Undoubtedly he would subdivide.

Jasper only hoped that seeing the results wouldn't kill him.

"We'll have to be out in thirty days," he said sadly. "You and me and Gray. We'll have to start over, but we'll do it together. I already signed the agreement. The money will be delivered sometime this afternoon. Now, if only the kidnapper would call with the drop-off—''

Marlene stopped him by throwing her arms around his neck. She was sobbing so hard she was shaking. That woman had some waterworks, he thought. He hugged her to him, only then noticing Reine standing in the doorway. From her expression, he figured she'd heard everything.

He also sensed something off with her.

He patted Marlene's back. ''Reine's here.'' Then, when his wife let go her stranglehold, he asked, ''Honey, where have you been?''

''Out looking for Gray myself.''

She probably had, though she couldn't have done it in the dead of night. He doubted she'd slept in either of her beds. He could only guess whose she had been in and how she'd gotten here. He knew she'd been driving his old rattler rather than her own car. But she was a grown woman. And he needn't be criticizing anyone else's behavior at this point.

So, instead, he said, ''You look tired.''

''I didn't get much sleep.''

''What about food?'' Marlene asked. ''Have you eaten?''

''Not today.''

''Me, neither. It's time we all broke bread together, don't you think? All of us. We need to fortify ourselves—''

The telephone ringing stopped Marlene's prattling.

All three stared at the instrument until it rang again. His heart in his throat, Jasper lunged for it and turned on the speaker phone.

Then, hands flat on his desk, as calmly as his heart would let him, he said, "Matlock."

"Anxious?" asked that sexless voice that he both hated and needed to hear.

"Sundown can't come soon enough for me."

"Good. That means you'll be prompt."

"Where?" Jasper demanded.

"The abandoned chile mill."

"Gray'll be there?"

"Bring the money in a set of saddlebags. Leave them on the stoop and get out. You'll be watched, so don't try anything. Once the money is counted—"

"Forget it. You want the money, you give me my son."

"You want your son, you'll do as I say. You leave the money and, after we make sure it's all there, we'll leave your boy at the mill."

Jasper knew when he was defeated. He couldn't chance Gray. Not now.

"All right."

The laugh at the other end made his skin crawl. He flashed a look at Marlene and Reine. Both women seemed to be holding their breath.

He'd leave the money as instructed, but he wouldn't go far, he decided. He'd retreat to a place up on the ridge where he could get a bead on whoever rode up to collect.

And if Gray wasn't with the pickup man, he would shoot the bastard dead.

REINE WAS SICK AT HEART. All the way back to the house, she'd tried to figure out what to say to her aunt and uncle, and in the end, had kept silent about what she knew.

For the first time since this horror story had begun, they stood united. She couldn't ruin what little hope they had by telling them Gray might already be dead. She couldn't think that way, either. Gray couldn't be dead.

He *wasn't!*

So why hadn't she and Cash been able to find him?

It was as if he'd just disappeared. They'd looked everywhere.

Or had they?

A vague memory from her childhood stirred—of a space dark and dank, isolated, the entrance nearly impossible to find, even when you knew it was supposed to be there somewhere.

The cave… They hadn't even thought of it!

Now that she had, a chill shuddered through her—she'd hated the place.

Even so, she had to admit that with its branching tunnels, the cave made a perfect refuge. Even if the person who'd likely shot Gray had tracked him to the entrance, Gray could have lost him, possibly even come out in any number of spots.

Not that she'd ever investigated far enough in to find one. Reine still remembered the confusing network of underground passages with distaste. She'd been inside only once, and that had been twenty years before.

Thinking she could cover more rough ground on a horse, she tacked up Gold Mine and loaded the saddlebags with some snack bars, a first-aid kit and a couple of flashlights with strong batteries. Then she filled a canteen with fresh water and secured it to the saddle.

As she rode out, Reine tried to visualize the entrance to the cave. Cash had been the one to find it, of course. The three of them had only gone inside together that once, though she suspected the boys might have returned without her.

If only Cash were with her. She could use his help and support about now. But after they'd given up their search that morning, he'd seemed distracted and eager to get away from her. He'd used the excuse of having some business or other he had to attend to. She'd been appalled that he could even now put business above Gray.

But she hadn't been much surprised.

Besides which, Cash hadn't taken her heartfelt-if-amateur analysis of his psyche where Uncle Jasper was concerned too well. He probably hadn't wanted to be around her after that.

Even so, before setting off, Reine had called him and left a message on his answering machine as to where she was headed. She couldn't help wanting to believe that, in the end, Cash really would come through for Gray.

And for her.

Her thoughts were so squarely centered on the man she loved and on what might have been between them that she was amazed when she suddenly realized how far she'd come. She also realized that another weather front was imminent as they passed the mouth of the box canyon.

Reine urged Gold Mine faster toward the hills that she and Cash had already searched that morning. On a small, windswept peak, she stopped and stared at the whole panorama spread out before her.

The lower hills were covered with chamiza and aspen that trembled with each gust. Behind them lay the nearly barren barrancas. In the distance were the *cerros*—hills—with soil too poor to sustain crops. And in between were the cottonwood-limned arroyos—deep chasms cut by the rivers that connected mountains to valleys and that were the lifeblood of this land.

Somewhere in all of that, she would find Gray.

Reine took Gold Mine as far as the terrain would allow the mare easy footing. When it became too difficult, she dismounted and secured the reins to a spindly aspen, then dug into the saddlebags. When the snack bars were stuffed into her jeans' pockets and flashlights clipped to her belt, she swung the canteen over one shoulder and, hoping she would have no need for it, the first-aid kit over the other.

Then she climbed over a ridge and started down an embankment toward a curve in the river that seemed familiar. Halfway down, she stopped to get her bearings and noted a rock outcropping off to the south, midway along the slope. The winds kicked up just then, rocking her. The air was heavy and thick. She glanced up at the ever-more-menacing sky and decided she'd better hurry.

Certain the jagged *peñasco* was familiar, she headed straight for it. But as she went, she tried not to be too discouraged wondering if a wounded man could really cross this rough terrain on his own. She reminded herself how tough Gray had always been.

There was no reason to believe otherwise now.

Reine's stomach quivered as she neared the outcropping, feeling more certain than ever that this was the place. And as she rounded the rock, she spotted the opening so cleverly concealed by Mother Nature that, if she hadn't known to look for it, she would have passed it right by.

The sky opened even before she got inside, rain plastering her shirt to her back.

She stood there for a moment, watching the torrent beat down, trying to shake off the sudden chill. A wind seemed to blow over her from inside the cave.

Plucking at the material sticking to her back, she turned toward the dark depths that she really didn't want to enter, took a deep breath and shouted, "Gray, it's Reine! If you can hear me, yell or something!"

As hard as she listened, she only managed to hear the splash of rain against rocks coming from the other side of the cave mouth. She'd have to go farther in.

Clicking on one of the lights that she left attached to her belt to keep both hands free, she moved deeper into the cave and tried not to let its narrowing confines bother her. Up ahead it would split in several directions, she remembered. The other time, they'd taken the far left fork.

She yelled again. "Gray! Can you hear me?" Her voice was hollow and scared sounding.

A moment later, it was time to choose. The left fork too quickly closed around her. A hundred yards in, another split presented itself. Again, she stayed to the left, remembering how the floor of the cave had risen if not the ceiling. Within minutes, she was stooped over, then on her hands and knees, with the swinging light illuminating the rock floor several yards ahead.

How far to go before she could breathe normally? Reine wondered.

Small, enclosed places still spooked her and she was a whole lot bigger than she had been the last time she'd tried this. Her stomach knotted and her skin crawled. She lifted the light and flashed it forward.

Ahead, the tunnel narrowed even more.

Reine would have liked nothing better than to turn back. She sat on her haunches, trying to decide whether or not to continue on and face her demons.

"Gray!" she called halfheartedly, suddenly feeling as if she were on a fool's errand. "It's Reine!"

A faint sound ahead took the decision away from her. A voice?

She scrambled forward on hands and knees, listening hard, hearing nothing more than her own breathing.

"Gray?" she called again.

And swore she heard something. Her name?

"Hold on, I'm coming!"

Rock walls were touching her so she had to keep her head bent as she drove forward, nearly having to get on her belly. The swinging light showed the tunnel widening into another alcove ahead. She sobbed with relief as the rock walls lifted away from her and she was able to get to her feet. She practically fell into the chamber, ecstatic at hearing footsteps that weren't her own.

"Gray, I found you."

"Sorry to disappoint you, sweetheart."

The voice wasn't Gray's.

Reine flashed the light upward, and was horrified when it revealed a familiar, churlish snarl.

JASPER HAD GIVEN THAT pocket watch of his the evil eye so many times in the last hour that Marlene was surprised it hadn't stopped ticking.

"Maybe you'd better call," she suggested again from her spot on the sofa.

This time, he nodded. "Maybe I'd better."

She was trying to stay calm, but considering the circumstances...

Sunset would be here all too soon.

Jasper swore under his breath as he waited for Bixler to come to the phone. Marlene wrapped her arms around her middle and held on as best she could.

"Bixler!" he finally said in a tight voice. "I expected your man to be here by now."

If only he would soften his tone, Marlene thought. Cajole the man instead of riling him. Why couldn't he learn to deal with people as he should?

"What do you mean there's been a hitch?"

Her breath caught in her chest. She staggered to her feet and toward her husband.

"Tomorrow will be too damn late!" Jasper yelled. "It has to be right now!"

Noticing her distress, Jasper pulled her to him and held on tight.

Marlene clutched at his shirt and tried to listen to the other end of the conversation. But all she could hear was the rushing of her own blood in her ears.

"Then you can take your money and..."

Trembling with rage, Jasper slammed the receiver into its cradle.

"I—I don't understand...."

"Neither do I. Bixler assured me he could have the money today." Cursing a blue streak, Jasper first hugged her, then let her go and raced toward his office. "I'm delivering what money I already have, anyway. Maybe a couple hundred thousand will buy us time."

Marlene was shaking as she watched him re-emerge from his office, saddlebags slung over one shoulder. He stopped briefly to kiss her, then flew out the front door.

She'd never before prayed so hard that he was right.

ACTING ON INSTINCT, Reine grabbed the leather strap from her left shoulder and swung her body and the canteen, all in a single, smooth motion.

Its impact when smacking the snarling man square in the throat jarred her whole arm. He gave a strangled oath, and in the beam bouncing from the light at her belt, she saw something go flying. From the sound of it, he'd just lost both his breath and his gun.

Wasting no time, she flew back the way she'd come.

"Stop, you bitch, or I'll shoot!"

"You've got to get your gun first," she muttered.

It seemed he already had, for she heard a scrabbling sound behind her. But no shots rang out. He must want her alive for something.

Her relief was short-lived. What felt like a vise clamped around one of her ankles.

He jerked and she fell.

Again, on instinct, she rolled to the side, counted—to make certain he was close enough—and on *three* struck out with her free foot. Her boot heel made contact, this time with a loud crunch.

"My nose!" he screamed. "I'll get you for this!"

But, adrenaline pumping, Reine was back on her knees and scrambling away fast, this time savoring the feel of the rock walls closing snuggly around her; her attacker was far bigger than she and would have a more difficult time getting through the tunnel. That should be good for a few seconds' head start, at least.

Even over her own labored breathing, she heard him squirming and cursing as he forced his way through.

Then the tunnel loosened its grip on her and she moved even faster...rushing to her feet...running in a stooped position...straightening barely long enough to catch her breath—when she was grabbed from behind, her mouth instantly covered so she couldn't yell out.

"Quietly," the man whispered in her ear even as he swung her into another tunnel.

CASH FLEW OUT OF THE Jaguar, cursing the fates and the weather that had delayed him. He sloshed through puddles rapidly disappearing into the sieve-like soil. When he got to the front door, he took a minute to pull himself together. His fingers tightened on the well-worn leather saddlebags he was carrying. He hadn't stepped foot in Jasper Matlock's house since he was a teenager, and then it had been without the old man's permission.

He wouldn't be doing so now, except...

Banging a fist against the door, he nearly shot right on through. Someone had left it open.

He could feel the surge of his vitals as he stepped inside the foyer, yelling, "Anyone home?"

There was no answer.

His pulse quickened. "Reine?" Where else would she be? He took another few steps.

And then he saw her. Marlene. She was sitting on the couch, head bowed, hands clasped before her. And she was rocking to some inner rhythm that scared him. He approached her carefully as he would a wild animal he didn't want to frighten away.

"Marlene," he said as gently as he could manage. He knelt before her. "It's me, Cash. Has something happened?"

She raised her head. Her face was grief-stricken, but her eyes were unnaturally dry, as if she'd already cried out her soul and had nothing left to give.

"My boy's going to die, Cash. I have to face it. Gray's going to die and I can't stop it. No one can, now."

"Yes, we can, with—"

"Jasper didn't get the money," she cried. "He did try. But at the last minute, Bixler didn't come through."

"Evan Bixler was going to give you the two million, no strings attached?"

He'd already considered Bixler's possible involvement in the kidnapping.

"One very big string," Marlene said. "The ranch. But something went wrong."

"Something's going right. Finally." Cash pulled the saddlebags from his shoulder and handed them to her. "I'm giving you the money."

"I don't understand. Just yesterday, you refused to buy my share—"

"Not buy. I'm giving it to you. Really, no strings attached."

Wonder and hope now shining on her face, she said, "Cash, I don't know how to thank you."

"No need. Gray is my brother, after all."

He rose and started to back away.

"Wait. Jasper's already gone to the mill to leave what money he could raise. And I have no idea where Reine has disappeared to. She left hours ago. Rode out on Gold Mine. She hasn't come back."

Which didn't sound good at all, Cash thought, a sick feeling filling him. She'd probably gone charging to the drop-off site, as well.

Marlene rose, saddlebags in hand. She held them out to him. "Would you take the money to the abandoned mill? Please. For Gray."

Cash nodded. He had a feeling Reine was there anyway, and he wasn't going to leave her to her own devices.

"I'll do it, Marlene," he promised. "For all of us."

THE LIGHT WAS ALREADY fading by the time Jasper got into position up on the ridge. Even as he raised his binoculars, he caught a hint of movement below.

He focused, but what he could see was limited by the deepening gloom and the drizzle that was coming down again. Nevertheless, he couldn't miss the man who rode straight up to the chile mill. There was something familiar about the horse. And about the figure who dismounted and went directly for the stoop and the saddlebags.

Jasper quickly checked the surrounding area to be certain. No sign of anyone else.

No Gray!

"Son of a bitch!" he muttered.

He'd stop the bastard from taking off. He'd torture the information from him about where he could find his son. And then he'd turn over what was left to the sheriff.

Trading the binoculars for his rifle, he hefted it to his shoulder and took aim even as the man got back to the horse. Fury and grief roiled together, but purpose steadied his weapon. Even as his chest squeezed tight, so did his finger on the trigger.

It was a direct hit.

The man flew back, his dark hat flying from his head, saddlebags falling to the ground—one set from each of his hands.

"What the hell?"

Plunging to his feet, Jasper grabbed up his binoculars. *Two sets of saddlebags.* And the horse was one of his own. Then he got a better look at the man on the ground, whose pale shirt was now stained dark with blood.

No wonder he'd seemed so familiar.

Bile rose up into Jasper's throat as the realization hit him.

He'd just shot his own son!

"Cash! Oh, my God, what have I done?"

Chapter Fourteen

"Gray," she said in barely more than a whisper. Reine hadn't said a word until they'd zigzagged through several tunnels and stopped in a chamber where she was certain the man Tobiah had identified as Lloyd Rynko wouldn't be able to find them. But she couldn't keep quiet any longer. "I was so scared for you." When she tried to hug him, he flinched. "How bad is it?"

"I'm alive."

But not looking too good, she decided after flicking on a flashlight and checking him out. His eyes were bright. She put her hand to his face. It was feverish. Half his shirt was stained red, and he was hugging his left arm to his side.

"You've lost so much blood. Sit down and let me tend to you."

"Gotta keep going or he'll catch up to us."

"Sit!" she hissed.

Even as Gray did as she demanded, Reine was rifling through the first-aid kit. She pulled out a couple of painkiller/fever reducers and an antibiotic. She handed over the pills and held the canteen for him. He couldn't seem to get enough water.

"How long ago were you shot?"

"Don't know. I've lost track of time down here in the dark. But it was just after dawn."

More than half a day.

With dread, she said, "I'd better take a look at that shoulder."

"You've gotten some doctoring skills I don't know about?"

"I'm not going to try removing a bullet with my teeth, if that's what's worrying you."

Gray's shoulder was a mess. She tried to detach herself as she cleaned him up with alcohol pads and got a better look at the wound. Fortunately, it wasn't as bad as she'd feared.

"Scar won't be too big," she guessed. "Just enough to impress the ladies. Grit your teeth so you don't yell."

As Reine cleaned the actual tear in his flesh and applied some antibiotic salve, Gray stiffened but didn't make a sound. Wanting to cry for him, she dressed the wound carefully.

"That's the best I can do."

Gray caught her hand. "Thanks, Reine. I should have known you wouldn't give up on me."

Tears sprang to her eyes. "Of course I wouldn't, you dope. Not any more than you would give up on me. We're family." Which reminded her… She took a big breath. "By the way, neither has Cash. We've been together on this."

They had been until now, anyway, and Gray didn't need to know anything else.

"'All for one,'" Gray murmured, sounding pleased if equally astounded. "I'll be damned."

She pulled out the snack bars from her jeans

pocket and handed him two. "Eat." Then she ripped open a third for herself. For the first time in days, she had a real appetite.

"Too bad snarl-boy followed you in here," she said, still keeping her voice low.

"I think he'd be long gone if he could only find his way out." Having finished the first bar, he started on the second. "He never got close to me."

"When was the last time you were in these tunnels?"

"Not since Cash...left. But we'd done enough exploring that I knew them like the back of my hand. Memory's pretty good. Didn't even need a flashlight."

"Which is good since you didn't have one anyway." She took another bite. "And I knew the two of you were sneaking out here without me!"

Gray didn't comment.

It was amazing that he was so alert, considering the wound. She touched the backs of her fingers to his forehead—he seemed a little cooler. And she swore his eyes didn't seem quite so bright. She took a swig of water to wash down the remains of her bar and handed him the canteen.

"Drink deep."

He emptied the container and she knew he would feel better for it. But well enough to get out of the tunnels and to someplace safe?

If they could get to Gold Mine, her mare could carry them both back to the house. But they still had Rynko to deal with and neither of them was packing a gun.

"So what's next?" she asked. "How do we get out of here alive?"

RAIN SPLATTERING HIM brought Cash instantly awake. *Vitally* awake. He was aware of a pain ripping through his chest like none he'd ever experienced.

"You're alive!"

He blinked and Jasper Matlock came into focus directly above him. Water was rolling off the old man's hat and directly into his face.

"Someone shot me," he groaned.

"Me. Didn't know it was you, though," Matlock said, sounding defensive. "Thought I had the kidnapper in my sights."

"Wait a minute...." Cash tried to rise, but the pain changed his mind. "You thought *I* was the kidnapper."

"Once a fool, always a fool. Let's see how bad that is." He quickly opened Cash's shirt and took a look. "It's a clean hit," he said, sounding approving of his own marksmanship.

Cash muttered, "What a relief."

"And you'll live."

Matlock was stuffing something inside his shirt that made Cash want to yowl. But not in front of the old man. He clenched his jaw against the pain instead.

"Gotta put a little pressure on it to get the bleeding to stop."

Cash nodded and drew on his reserves. He found a place in the far back reaches of his mind to put the pain. He'd take it out and examine it later.

The wind whipped over him, making him shiver despite himself. While the drizzle had stopped, strong currents of air still gusted around them. Their horses shifted around and whinnied nervously.

"Where's Reine?" Cash grunted.

"Back at the house, I expect."

"No." Cash was getting the worst feeling.... "What does she have herself into this time?"

"You sound like you care."

"Always did, despite what you assumed."

Ignoring that, Matlock asked, "Think you can get up?"

Cash rose as far as his elbows before noticing that the man was holding out a hand. Reluctantly, he took it and struggled to his feet, which gave him his first close-up look at his biological father since reaching adulthood. He could almost swear that regret crossed the man's features.

Then Matlock ended the moment by demanding, "What the hell did you think you were doing down here anyhow? Why'd you mess with the saddlebags?"

Cash couldn't believe it. The old buzzard had shot him and was now putting the blame on him, as well.

"I was leaving the ransom," he replied stiffly. "I didn't see any reason for the kidnapper to get a bonus. Any sign of him, by the way? He should be along any time to collect."

"I'm right here," came a familiar voice from behind them.

They'd been so busy arguing, they hadn't heard anyone approach.

Cash whipped around, saying, "Valdez, *you?*" And saw that Matlock's neighbor was holding a gun on them. "Why?"

"Simple. This land was stolen from my daddy. My family dates back nearly two hundred years in this valley. We had legal claim through my ancestors who settled the territory. But our name was Valdez, and Marlene's Anglo papa had friends in high places.''

Cash knew such unfortunate things had happened throughout the Southwest, but Gray had done nothing wrong. It wasn't even the old man's fault.

"How was taking my boy gonna get you the river property?" Matlock's tone was thick with derision.

Even in the deepening gloom, Cash could see the disdain on Sam Valdez's face.

"It's complicated, as Abreu here can tell you."

"Whoa! Don't try to connect me to the kidnapping. Where is Gray, anyway?"

To Cash's frustration, Valdez didn't answer, rather spoke directly to Matlock. "Abreu started it all by making me think I could get the land back. He came to me with a deal—he'd finance the property, which I would then turn over to him, while retaining water rights forever. But you weren't selling. Then I figured you would if I could make you need the money badly enough."

"To save my boy."

"And he figured I was going to provide him with the means to buy the land from you," Cash volunteered. "Not that I agreed, once things got so complicated. I wouldn't be surprised if Valdez meant to double-cross me all along and figure a way to keep the land, not just the water rights."

"You'd be correct on that score. I decided I could have not only the land but your two million bucks, once Jasper agreed to sell. I'd give it to him, then get it right back in ransom money."

"Only I'm not gonna agree—not ever!"

Valdez's laugh raised the small hairs on the back of Cash's neck.

Waving his gun, he said, "Then it's time for Plan B."

"Which would be?"

"This is so perfect. I can see the headlines now: Father and Son Shoot Each Other to Death. Grieving Widow Takes Comfort in Neighbor's Arms. That way I get the ransom, the land, and not one, but two bonuses! Even more money, and the woman that should have been mine in the first place."

"Marlene would never give you the time of day!"

"She already has."

"Why, you—"

Matlock started to lunge for the other man, but Cash shoved him out of the way even as Valdez's gun discharged.

REINE'S HEART DRUMMED as Lloyd Rynko came close enough that she could hear him cursing. Having no flashlight of his own, he was blindly shuffling through the tunnels, still trying to find her—or find his way out. By calling for Gray several times, she'd led him in their direction, if not as quickly as she might have liked. She would have loved to leave him and find one of the other exits—thereby avoiding any unexpected and potentially deadly encounters—but, once on the surface, they would have had to backtrack too far and in too bad weather for an injured man. Besides, Rynko had to be stopped before he killed someone.

The plan was Gray's and it would work.

Figuring Rynko was now close enough for them to get his attention, Reine turned on one of the flashlights and flung it down a tunnel, then pulled back into a nearby opening even as a shot rang out. The whine of the bullet scraped up her spine. She held her breath and heard Rynko run toward the light close to her hiding place.

Gray was waiting to trip him up. Literally.

The moment he sent Rynko sprawling, Reine flashed the second light directly into the man's eyes, blinding him long enough for Gray to get the drop on him. Using his good arm, Gray landed a chop across the back of the guy's neck. Rynko tried to rise anyway, but Reine wiped the snarl right off his face by smacking his broken, bloody nose with the now empty canteen. Just enough weight to do the trick, she decided, when she heard the gun clatter to the rock floor for the second time.

Gray hooked an arm across Rynko's throat.

"Handy little weapon," Reine said of the canteen. Then, collecting Rynko's gun, she pointed it directly at him. "I wouldn't move if I were you."

Blood drizzled down his chin. "Like you even know how to use that without hitting the wrong man," he said in a strange, nasal voice.

"Try her," Gray dared him. "I taught her to shoot when she was twelve. She could knock the eye out of a snake at a hundred yards."

"Now don't go exaggerating," Reine warned him. "It was probably only fifty yards."

Rynko cursed and gave her the evil eye, but he didn't try anything.

"I've got him covered," Reine said gleefully. "Tie him up."

Gray had taken the leather strap from the first-aid kit and had attached it to a natural fissure in the tunnel wall. Holding the other end, he'd used it to trip Rynko. Now he used the line to secure the man's arms behind his back. Reine could see that Gray was having a bit of trouble using his left hand, but he was still doing a creditable job and wasn't complaining.

"The canteen," Gray said.

She tossed it to him and he caught it deftly with his right hand. Detaching that strap as well, he bound Rynko's legs together with it.

"You wouldn't want to tell us who you're working for, would you?" Reine asked.

"If you'll let me go...."

"We'll let you testify," she returned. "Maybe you can make some kind of deal."

"Screw a deal! I'll take my chances."

"Your call."

"My call? Then let me tell you what I'm going to do to you when I get my hands around your scrawny neck—"

Gray slapped a hand over the man's mouth. "Any tape left in that first-aid kit?" Gray asked.

"Some." She dug into the leather bag and pulled out what was left of the small roll.

"You'll have to do the honors."

Handing him the gun, she pulled a length of tape from its roll even while considering whether or not the man would be able to breathe. She had broken his nose, after all.

"What's that for?" Rynko demanded.

"So your caterwauling won't scare the lizards," she told him as she planted the tape across his open mouth.

Gray rose, saying, "Let's see how *you* like being left in the dark, tied up and gagged."

"Mmmph."

He seemed to be breathing well enough.

"Don't worry." Reine fetched the second flashlight that she'd tossed. No way was she going to make it easier on him. "We'll send the sheriff out here to get you...eventually. Just hope he can find his way around these tunnels better than you could." She put an arm around Gray's waist. "C'mon, cousin, get me out of here fast. I always did hate small, dark places."

She couldn't be happier about Gray.

Cash was another matter. She didn't know how she felt about him not having been around to see the story played out.

CASH HAD MADE THE unfortunate mistake of striking Valdez with his wounded shoulder. The gun went spinning off into the brush, but the pain put him into enough shock to give the other man the advantage. He ran.

That was when he noticed Matlock was down, unmoving.

In a haze of pain that paralyzed him for the moment, Cash watched Valdez scoop up the saddlebags and open all of the flaps. He then started transferring money from one set of leather pouches to the other. Haste made him sloppy and he dropped some of the bills.

Then a gust of wind confounded him, sucking a bunch more from his hands. There were plenty more where those came from, but Valdez seemed determined not to lose a single one.

His greed was his undoing.

The rancher grew careless as he tried to retrieve

the money, fumbling with the bags. They dropped from his hands, sliding open to the wind. A fistful of hundreds went spiraling up the canyon.

"No!" Valdez yelled, grasping at them.

His pain receding enough to let him function, Cash went after the man.

Valdez was so caught up in recovering the money, that he didn't see the threat until Cash was upon him. He swung out, but Cash ducked, coming back with a hard right to the gut. The rancher doubled over, then tried to head-butt Cash, who was able to dance out of his way and, as Valdez surged on past, managed to kick him in the backside for good measure.

Valdez stumbled over the saddlebags, his feet tangling in the leathers, money shooting out around him like feathers released from a ripped pillow.

Wind howled down the canyon and sucked the bills into a vortex around him.

Cash plunged an arm through the paper flurry and grabbed Valdez by the throat. In seconds, he pinned him, with his knees to the man's chest and right arm, so he couldn't do any further damage.

"Where's Gray?" Cash demanded.

"I don't know."

Cash started to squeeze. "The truth?"

Valdez gasped, "Gone! That trigger-happy fool Rynko shot him, then Skinner scurried off like the coward he is. I told them no violence!"

So Skinner *had* been involved. It had been *his* cigar Cash had found, not Bixler's.

"'No violence,'" he echoed. "That's why you were talking about killing me and Matlock?"

"Wishful thinking," Valdez gasped. "I just wanted what was due me, is all."

Paper money still fluttered around them as Cash let go of the man's throat.

Rising, he ignored his own dizziness and the warmth dripping down his chest to check on Matlock, to see how badly he was hurt. He was just stooping over the old man when he heard a scuffle and realized his mistake in turning his back on Valdez. The rancher was coming for him, a huge rock in hand.

Cash rolled out of the way even as a shot rang out. Pain searing his chest and arm from the action, he blinked and saw Valdez clutching his empty hand. Then he whipped around to see who had wielded the weapon. Even in the near dark, he couldn't miss the two riders on the pale Palomino.

His heart lifted.

Reine was holding a gun on Valdez, and a live if sick-looking Gray was hanging on behind her.

"Looks like we got here just in time," Reine said. She waved the gun at Valdez. "Get down on the ground before I shoot you between the eyes like the snake you are."

Gray slid off the horse first. "Hey, Cash, still can't keep outta trouble, huh?"

"Back at you."

Reine dismounted, her eyes going wide when she saw Matlock. "Uncle Jasper... He isn't...dead?"

Matlock groaned and finally opened his eyes. "I'm not ready for the grave yet, girl." He sat up, holding his head. "Just got a bump is all. So don't go planning my funeral." Then he noticed Gray and struggled to his feet. "Son, thank God we got you back!"

The little energy he had left draining from him, Cash watched as Matlock went to Gray and threw his arms around him. He looked away, content to let God take the credit. Gray was all that mattered.

But a moment later, he felt another presence at his side. The woman he loved touched his good arm.

"What happened here?" Reine asked, looking around in amazement.

Cash blinked and focused as best he could. The fortune he'd worked so hard to make was spread out over the canyon before him. Money was everywhere, the bills plastered to the wet ground and hillside and trees—all but for those being skittered over the ridge by the wind. It wouldn't be long before everything was just plain gone.

The thing about it was that he didn't give a damn.

Dizziness swept through him and he thought maybe he'd lost too much blood. "It's all a cosmic joke," he muttered.

Then it got too dark to see anything at all.

Tuesday

CASH AWOKE FEELING groggy. And confused. Darkness surrounded him, but he knew he was inside somewhere, out of the elements. And the room had a medicinal smell.

As his eyes adjusted, he made out curtains all around him and a patch of light under and over one side. He stirred and tried to move. Pain—and a board and needle attached to his arm—kept him still.

"The doctors say you'll live," came a soft voice out of the dark.

Reine. How long had she been there, watching over him?

"That's a good thing, I guess. I thought maybe I was bound to bleed to death."

She snapped on a nightlight. "Now, would I have allowed that?"

He vaguely remembered passing out and Reine reviving him long enough to get him on the horse he'd ridden out from the barn, followed by more blank spaces. Then, back at the house, there had been a flurry of noise and calls for an ambulance and the sheriff. And Marlene had been weeping.

"Gray?"

"He's doing just fine," she assured him.

Then it wasn't all for nothing.

He could feel her breath on his face as she leaned over the hospital bed toward him, careful not to touch him, as if she feared she would put him in more pain. Cash could care less. Reine could touch him to her heart's content. She stirred him as always and his wanting her grew stronger than the pain.

She drew so close, her mouth was within striking distance.

He reached out with his good hand and stroked her cheek with his knuckles. She closed her eyes and kissed his hand. He couldn't help himself. Pulling her head toward his, he caught her lips in a soft kiss. She sighed and the sound sang through his heart.

"How long have I been here?" he asked.

"Only a few hours in this room. They had to patch your tough hide, first. So, how bad do you feel?"

"Like I was run over by a horse."

"Thank God *that* didn't happen," she murmured. "When you went out on me, and I saw all that blood…you scared me real bad."

"That makes us even then," he admitted, reaching

out to touch her beautiful face. "You scared me when I arrived with the money and you weren't at the house. All kinds of crazy thoughts went through my mind."

"Sounds like a mutual admiration society," Reine said. "So what are you going to do about it this time?"

"What do you want me to do?" he asked, hardly able to get out the words, fearing they would be the wrong ones. "Last time I checked, you didn't like much about me."

"Maybe things have changed. Actually, you changed. Or maybe you just went back to being the Cash I grew up with. You came through for Gray in the end. I should have trusted that you would."

"What about Matlock?" he asked, testing her, wanting to be sure they were on the same page—as in a permanent relationship. Jasper Matlock was still a major obstacle. "He'd hate our being together."

"I'm not so sure of that, Cash. I think the two of you must have settled something between yourselves. He was actually worried about your recovery."

Cash didn't even know how he was supposed to feel about that.

One relationship at a time, he thought.

"Besides," she said, "I've done some thinking about that, as well. I just refuse to choose. I can love as many people as I want and I refuse to lose any of them because they don't get along."

"You love me?"

"I always have, Cash. I've never loved any other man."

She loved him. She wasn't going to give up on him. Cash wondered how he'd gotten so lucky.

Now, how was he supposed to tell her he wasn't quite the catch he had been twenty-four hours ago?

"I guess we could always live on that trust fund of yours till I can get back on my feet," he mused aloud.

"That trust fund is history. It was an exaggeration in a little girl's mind, anyway."

"Then the playing field really is leveled," he told her, watching for her reaction. "We're both pretty much busted. Working stiffs."

"You're broke? As in nothing left? You knowingly gave up everything for Gray?"

She sounded so shocked, he worried that she wasn't the same Reine he remembered.

"It makes that much of a difference to you?"

"It means everything to me. Far more than if you could easily have afforded to give it away."

"I still own the business, which is rock solid," he assured her. "Or will when I get two million dollars together. Payback," he said, not wanting to elaborate. "I'll just be strapped for cash for a long while. I may have lost most of my assets, but I've gained a brother."

And, it seemed, *her*.

"Would you just propose already!" demanded an impatient voice from the other side of the curtain. "Don't you know there are sick and injured people who need their rest in this hospital?"

Cash reached over to jerk open the curtain. Gray grinned at him from the other bed.

Unable to say the thing that was in his heart—that he was thankful Gray was alive—he asked, "Do I look as lousy as you do?"

"Worse. So are you serious about marrying this woman or not?"

"She's the only woman I've ever loved or wanted to marry," he told his brother.

"What about you, Reine?" Gray asked. "Will you marry this numbskull or not?"

She frowned at Cash. "You love me?"

"You know I do."

"I know no such thing unless you tell me."

"All right. I love you. Now what about the proposal?"

"Does it count coming from him?"

Cash grinned. "'All for one and one for all.'"

"Then, yes," she told Gray. "I'll marry him!"

Grinning like a fool now, Cash pulled the curtain back in place so he could kiss Reine in privacy.

Some things, he was not willing to share.

Epilogue

"'A cosmic joke' is right," Alex said when Zoe had finished telling her tale. "Two greedy men nearly impoverish themselves to see that someone they love is safe, and then all that money they stepped on so many people to make over the years gets blown away for nothing."

Zoe sat up straighter. "Not for nothing. Remember, Cash got a lot out of the experience—a relationship with his brother and a woman who loved him. Not that he didn't need some help along the way." She patted the thick file. "Family counseling. Marlene Matlock even convinced her husband they *all* needed to participate. Together."

"And old Jasper agreed?"

"When she threatened to leave him, he did."

Alex was impressed. Love did seem to be the emotion with the most muscle. It made people do strange things against their very nature.

"Did Cash ever get his company back on solid footing?"

"Eventually, if on a more modest scale. His values changed. He had someone to live with and love, after all. And Matlock was able to recuperate some of his losses, as well, since Cash was no longer out to destroy him. Maybe someday he can admit to his true feelings for the son he'd denied.''

''If he has them.''

When she said, ''People don't always recognize what's in their hearts, let alone express it,'' Alex figured she must have some personal experience in that area herself.

Zoe Declue had lots of little facets that interested him, and Alex vowed that someday, he would learn everything there was to know about her.

EXTRA! EXTRA!

**The book all your favorite authors
are raving about is finally here!**

**The 1999 Harlequin and Silhouette
coupon book.**

Each page is alive with savings that can't be beat!

**Getting this incredible coupon book is
as easy as 1, 2, 3.**

1. During the months of November and December 1999 buy
   any 2 Harlequin or Silhouette books.

2. Send us your name, address and 2 proofs of purchase (cash
   receipt) to the address below.

3. Harlequin will send you a coupon book worth $10.00 off
   future purchases of Harlequin or Silhouette books in 2000.

Send us 3 cash register receipts as proofs of purchase and
we will send you 2 coupon books worth a total saving of
$20.00 (limit of 2 books per customer).

Saving money has never been this easy.

Please allow 4-6 weeks for delivery. Offer expires December 31, 1999.

I accept your offer! Please send me (a) coupon booklet(s):

Name: _____

Address: _____ City: _____

State/Prov.: _____ Zip/Postal Code: _____

Send your name and address, along with your cash register receipts as
proofs of purchase, to:

In the U.S.: Harlequin Books, P.O. Box 9057, Buffalo, N.Y. 14269

In Canada: Harlequin Books, P.O. Box 622, Fort Erie, Ontario L2A 5X3

Order your books and accept this coupon offer through our web site
http://www.romance.net
Valid in U.S. and Canada only.   PHQ4994

HARLEQUIN®
Makes any time special ™

WIN A DREAM

In celebration of Harlequin®'s golden anniversary

Enter to win a *dream!* You could win:

- A luxurious trip for two to *The Renaissance Cottonwoods Resort* in Scottsdale, Arizona, or

- A bouquet of flowers once a week for a year from **FTD**, or

- A $500 shopping spree, or

- A fabulous bath & body gift basket, including **K-tel's** *Candlelight and Romance* 5-CD set.

Look for **WIN A DREAM** flash on specially marked Harlequin® titles by Penny Jordan, Dallas Schulze, Anne Stuart and Kristine Rolofson in October 1999*.

RENAISSANCE. COTTONWOODS RESORT
SCOTTSDALE, ARIZONA

Amnesia...
an unknown danger...
a burning desire.

With

HARLEQUIN®

I N T R I G U E®

you're just

A MEMORY AWAY

from passion, danger...and love!

**Look for all the books in this
exciting miniseries:**

**#527 ONE TEXAS NIGHT
by Sylvie Kurtz**
August 1999

**#531 TO SAVE HIS BABY
by Judi Lind**
September 1999

**#536 UNDERCOVER DAD
by Charlotte Douglas**
October 1999

A MEMORY AWAY—where remembering
the truth becomes a matter of life,
death...and love!

Available wherever Harlequin books are sold.

COMING NEXT MONTH

#533 STOLEN MOMENTS by B.J. Daniels
The McCord Family Countdown

Sexy cowboy Seth Gantry "kidnapped" Olivia McCord to save her
life, but his reluctant hostage refused to believe him—until their safe
house exploded. Now, in a race against time, Seth's the only man she
can trust. Determined to resist her allure, Seth vowed to keep her—
and his heart—safe at all costs....

#534 MIDNIGHT CALLER by Ruth Glick writing as Rebecca York
43 Light St.

Meg Faulkner is on a mission—one she can't remember. Inside the
confines of Glenn Bridgman's military-like estate, unsure of who is
friend and who is foe, she must fight to evoke the memories that will
set her free—and resist the temptation of the intensely desirable
Glenn. But when the memories come, will Meg be able to escape with
her heart intact?

#535 HIS ONLY SON by Kelsey Roberts
The Landry Brothers

Born and raised in Montana as the oldest of seven sons, Sam Landry
knew the importance of family. He wanted nothing more than to keep
the son he had come to love as his own—until he discovered the boy's
real mother was alive. Finding the alluring Callie Walters proved
dangerous—someone would kill to keep the truth a secret. But Sam
was determined to keep his son—and the woman he had come to
love—safe....

#536 UNDERCOVER DAD by Charlotte Douglas
A Memory Away...

FBI agent Stephen Chandler knows he and his ex-partner,
Rachel Goforth, are in danger, but he can't remember who's trying to
kill them or why—though Stephen can vividly recall his attraction to
the sensual Rachel. But when Rachel's daughter is kidnapped, nothing
can stop him from tracking a killer—especially when he learns her
child is also his....

Look us up on-line at: http://www.romance.net